STORIES FROM AIRLESS WASTES
AND UNCHARTED WORLDS

CHARLIE'S LAW

A seventeen-year-old orphan from outer space
turns out to be the galaxy's destructive weapon.

DAGGER OF THE MIND

A scientist goes berserk and imprisons Kirk in the
dread "Machine of Loneliness."

BALANCE OF TERROR

An outlaw planet suddenly imperils the safety of
the whole galaxy.

THE UNREAL McCOY

A strange monster that can change its shape at
will stalks the crew of the Enterprise.

AND OTHER TALES
OF INTERGALACTIC ADVENTURE FROM
STAR TREK

Star Trek

ADAPTED BY JAMES BLISH

BASED ON THE EXCITING NEW NBC-TV SERIES
CREATED BY GENE RODDENBERRY

BANTAM BOOKS
TORONTO · NEW YORK · LONDON

STAR TREK

A Bantam Book / published January 1967

2nd printing

3rd printing

4th printing

Published simultaneously in the United States and Canada

Bantam Books are published by Bantam Books, Inc., a subsidiary
of Grosset & Dunlap, Inc. Its trade-mark, consisting of the words
"Bantam Books" and the portrayal of a bantam, is registered in the
United States Patent Office and in other countries. Marca Registrada.
Bantam Books, Inc., 271 Madison Avenue, New York, N.Y. 10016.

PRINTED IN THE UNITED STATES OF AMERICA

to Harlan Ellison
    who was right all the time

Contents

★★★★★★★★★

Charlie's Law

☆☆

Though as Captain of the starship *Enterprise* James Kirk
had the final authority over four hundred officers and
crewmen, plus a small and constantly shifting population of passengers, and though in well more than twenty
years in space he had had his share of narrow squeaks,
he was firmly of the opinion that no single person ever
gave him more trouble than one seventeen-year-old boy.

Charles Evans had been picked up from a planet
called Thasus after having been marooned there for
fourteen years, the sole survivor of the crash of his
parents' research vessel. He was rescued by the survey
ship *Antares,* a transport about a tenth of the size of
the *Enterprise*, and subsequently transferred to Kirk's
ship, wearing hand-me-down clothes and carrying all the
rest of his possessions in a dufflebag.

The officers of the *Antares* who brought him aboard
the *Enterprise* spoke highly of Charlie's intelligence,
eagerness to learn, intuitive grasp of engineering matters—"He could run the *Antares* himself if he had to"—
and his sweetness of character; but it struck Kirk
that they were almost elbowing each other aside to praise
him, and that they were in an unprecedented hurry to
get back to their own cramped ship, without even so
much as begging a bottle of brandy.

Charlie's curiosity had certainly been obvious from those first moments, though he showed some trepidation, too—which was not surprising, considering his long and lonely exile. Kirk assigned Yeoman Rand to take him to his quarters. It was at this point that Charlie stunned her and everyone else present by asking Kirk honestly:

"Is that a girl?"

Leonard McCoy, the ship's surgeon, checked Charlie from top to toe and found him in excellent physical condition: no traces of malnutrition, of exposure, of hardship of any sort; truly remarkable for a boy who'd had to fend for himself on a strange world from the age of three. On the other hand, it was reasonable to suppose that fourteen years later, Charlie would either be in good shape, or dead; he would have had to come to terms with his environment within the first few years.

Charlie was not very communicative about this puzzle, though he asked plenty of questions himself—he seemed earnestly to want to know all the right things to do, and even more urgently, to be liked, but the purport of some of McCoy's questions apparently baffled him.

No, nobody had survived the crash. He had learned English by talking to the memory banks on the ship; they still worked. No, the Thasians hadn't helped him; there were no Thasians. At first he had eaten stores from the wreck; then he had found some other . . . things, growing around.

Charlie then asked to see the ship's rule book. On the *Antares,* he said, he hadn't done or said all the right things. When that happened, people got angry; he got angry, too. He didn't like making the same mistake twice.

"I feel the same way," McCoy told him. "But you can't rush such matters. Just keep your eyes open, and when in doubt, smile and say nothing. It works very nicely."

Charlie returned McCoy's grin, and McCoy dismissed

him with a swat on the rump, to Charlie's obvious astonishment.

McCoy brought the problem up again on the bridge with Kirk and his second-in-command, Mr. Spock. Yeoman Rand was there working on a duty roster, and at once volunteered to leave; but since she had seen as much of Charlie as anyone had, Kirk asked her to stay. Besides, Kirk was fond of her, though he fondly imagined that to be a secret even from her.

"Earth history is full of cases where a small child managed to survive in a wilderness," McCoy went on.

"I've read some of your legends," said Spock, who was native to a nonsolar planet confusingly called Vulcan. "They all seem to require a wolf to look after the infants."

"What reason would the boy have to lie, if there *were* Thasians?"

"Nevertheless there's some evidence that there were, at least millennia ago," Spock said. "The first survey reported some highly sophisticated artifacts. And conditions haven't changed on Thasus for at least three million years. There might well be *some* survivors."

"Charlie says there aren't," Kirk said.

"His very survival argues that there are. I've checked the library computer record on Thasus. There isn't much, but one thing it does say: 'No edible plant life.' He simply had to have had some kind of help."

"I think you're giving him less credit than he deserves," McCoy said.

"For the moment let's go on that assumption," Kirk said. "Mr. Spock, work out a briefing program for young Charlie. Give him things to do—places to be. If we keep him busy until we get to Colony Five, experienced educators will take him over, and in the meantime, he should leave us with relative calm aboard...Yeoman Rand, what do you think of our problem child?"

"Wellll," she said. "Maybe I'm prejudiced. I wasn't going to mention this, but...he followed me down the corridor yesterday and offered me a vial of perfume.

My favorite, too; I don't know how he knew it. There's none in the ship's stores, I'm sure of that."

"Hmm," McCoy said.

"I was just going to ask him where he got it, when he swatted me on the rump. After that I made it my business to be someplace else."

There was an outburst of surprised laughter, quickly suppressed.

"Anything else?" Kirk said.

"Nothing important. Did you know that he can do card tricks?"

"Now, where would he have learned that?" Spock demanded.

"I don't know, but he's very good. I was playing solitaire in the rec room when he came in. Lieutenant Uhura was playing 'Charlie is my darling' and singing, and at first he seemed to think she was mocking him. When he saw she didn't mean it personally, he came over to watch me, and he seemed to be puzzled that I couldn't make the game come out. So he made it come out for me—without even touching the cards, I'd swear to that. When I showed I was surprised, he picked up the cards and did a whole series of tricks with them, good ones. The best sleight-of-hand I've ever seen. He said one of the men on the *Antares* taught him how. He was enjoying all the attention, I could tell that, but I didn't want to encourage him too much myself. Not after the swatting incident."

"He got *that* trick from me, I'm afraid," McCoy said.

"No doubt he did," Kirk said. "But I think I'd better talk to him, anyhow."

"Fatherhood becomes you, Jim," McCoy said, grinning.

"Dry up, Bones. I just don't want him getting out of hand, that's all."

Charlie shot to his feet the moment Kirk entered his cabin; all his fingers, elbows, and knees seemed to bend the wrong way. Kirk had barely managed to nod when he burst out: "I didn't do anything!"

"Relax, Charlie. Just wanted to find out how you're getting along."

"Fine. I . . . I'm supposed to ask you why I shouldn't—I don't know how to explain it."

"Try saying it straight out, Charlie," Kirk said. "That usually works."

"Well, in the corridor . . . I talked to . . . when Janice . . . when Yeoman Rand was . . ." Abruptly, setting his face, he took a quick step forward and slapped Kirk on the seat. "I did that and she didn't like it. She said you'd explain it to me."

"Well," Kirk said, trying hard not to smile, "it's that there are things you can do with a lady, and things you can't. Uh, the fact is, there's no right way to hit a lady. Man to man is one thing, man to woman is something else. Do you understand?"

"I don't know. I guess so."

"If you don't, you'll just have to take my word for it for the time being. In the meantime, I'm having a schedule worked out for you, Charlie. Things to do, to help you learn all the things you missed while you were marooned on Thasus."

"That's very nice, for you to do that for me," Charlie said. He seemed genuinely pleased. "Do you like me?"

That flat question took Kirk off guard. "I don't know," he said equally flatly. "Learning to like people takes time. You have to watch what they do, try to understand them. It doesn't happen all at once."

"Oh," Charlie said.

"Captain Kirk," Lieutenant Uhura's voice broke in over the intercom.

"Excuse me, Charlie . . . Kirk here."

"Captain Ramart of the *Antares* is on D channel. Must speak to you directly."

"Right. I'll come up to the bridge."

"Can I come too?" Charlie said as Kirk switched out.

"I'm afraid not, Charlie. This is strictly ship's business."

"I won't disturb anybody," Charlie said. "I'll stay out of the way."

The boy's need for human company was touching, no matter how awkwardly he went about it. There were many years of solitude to be made up for. "Well, all right," Kirk said. "But only when you have my permission. Agreed?"

"Agreed," Charlie said eagerly. He followed Kirk out like a puppy.

On the bridge, Lieutenant Uhura, her Bantu face intent as a tribal statue's, was asking the microphone: "Can you boost your power, *Antares?* We are barely reading your transmission."

"We are at full output, *Enterprise,*" Ramart's voice said, very distant and hashy. "I must speak with Captain Kirk at once."

Kirk stepped up to the station and picked up the mike. "Kirk here, Captain Ramart."

"Captain, thank goodness. We're just barely in range. I've got to warn—"

His voice stopped. There was nothing to be heard from the speaker now but stellar static—not even a carrier wave.

"See if you can get them back," Kirk said.

"There's nothing to get, Captain," Lieutenant Uhura said, baffled. "They aren't transmitting any more."

"Keep the channel open."

Behind Kirk, Charlie said quietly: "That was an old ship. It wasn't very well constructed."

Kirk stared at him, and then swung toward Spock's station.

"Mr. Spock, sweep the transmission area with probe sensors."

"I've got it," Spock said promptly. "But it's fuzzy. Unusually so even for this distance."

Kirk turned back to the boy. "What happened, Charlie? Do you know?"

Charlie stared back at him, with what seemed to be uneasy defiance. "I don't know," he said.

"The fuzzy area is spreading out," Spock reported.

"I'm getting some distinct pips now along the edges. Debris, undoubtedly."

"But no *Antares*?"

"Captain Kirk, that *is* the *Antares*," Spock said quietly. "No other interpretation is possible. Clearly, she blew up."

Kirk continued to hold Charlie's eye. The boy looked back.

"I'm sorry it blew up," Charlie said. He seemed uneasy, but nothing more than that. "But I won't miss them. They weren't very nice. They didn't like me. I could tell."

There was a long, terribly tense silence. At last Kirk carefully unclenched his fists.

"Charlie," he said, "one of the first things you're going to have to get rid of is that damned cold-bloodedness. Or self-centeredness, or whatever it is. Until that gets under control, you're going to be less than half human."

And then, he stopped. To his embarrassed amazement, Charlie was crying.

"He what?" Kirk said, looking up from his office chair at Yeoman Rand. She was vastly uncomfortable, but she stuck to her guns.

"He made a pass at me," she repeated. "Not in so many words, no. But he made me a long, stumbling speech. He wants me."

"Yeoman, he's a seventeen-year-old boy."

"Exactly," the girl said.

"All this because of a swat?"

"No, sir," she said. "Because of the speech. Captain, I've seen that look before; *I'm* not seventeen. And if something isn't done, sooner or later I'm going to have to hold Charlie off, maybe even swat him myself, and not on the fanny, either. That wouldn't be good for him. I'm his first love and his first crush and the first woman he ever saw and..." She caught her breath. "Captain, that's a great deal for anyone to have to handle, even one item at a time. All at once, it's murder.

And he doesn't understand the usual put-offs. If I have to push him off in a way he does understand, there may be trouble. Do you follow me?"

"I think so, Yeoman," Kirk said. He still could not quite take the situation seriously. "Though I never thought I'd wind up explaining the birds and the bees to anybody, not at my age. But I'll send for him right now."

"Thank you, sir." She went out. Kirk buzzed for Charlie. He appeared almost at once, as though he had been expecting something of the sort.

"Come in, Charlie, sit down."

The boy moved to the chair opposite Kirk's desk and sat down, as if settling into a bear trap. As before, he beat Kirk to the opening line.

"Janice," he said. "Yeoman Rand. It's about her, isn't it?"

Damn the kid's quickness! "More or less. Though it's more about you."

"I won't hit her like that any more. I promised."

"There's more to it than that," Kirk said. "You've got some things to learn."

"Everything I do or say is wrong," Charlie said desperately. "I'm in the way. Dr. McCoy won't show me the rules. I don't know what I am or what I'm supposed to be, or even *who*. And I don't know why I hurt so much inside all the time—"

"I do, and you'll live," Kirk said. "There's nothing wrong with you that hasn't gone haywire inside every human male since the model came out. There's no way to get over it, around it, or under it; you just have to live through it, Charlie."

"But, it's like I'm wearing my insides outside. I go around bent over all the time. Janice—Yeoman Rand— she wants to give me away to someone else. Yeoman Lawton. But she's just a, just a, well, she doesn't even smell like a girl. Nobody else on the ship is like Janice. I don't want anybody else."

"It's normal," Kirk said gently. "Charlie, there are a

million things in the universe you can have. There are also about a hundred million that you can't. There's no fun in learning to face that, but you've got to do it. That's how things are."

"I don't like it," Charlie said, as if that explained everything.

"I don't blame you. But you have to hang on tight and survive. Which reminds me: the next thing on your schedule is unarmed defense. Come along to the gym with me and we'll try a few falls. Way back in Victorian England, centuries ago, they had a legend that violent exercise helped keep one's mind off women. I've never known it to work, myself, but anyhow let's give it a try."

Charlie was incredibly clumsy, but perhaps no more so than any other beginner. Ship's Officer Sam Ellis, a member of McCoy's staff, clad like Kirk and Charlie in work-out clothes, was patient with him.

"That's better. Slap the mat when you go down, Charlie. It absorbs the shock. Now, again."

Ellis dropped of his own initiative to the mat, slapped it, and rolled gracefully up onto his feet. "Like that."

"I'll never learn," Charlie said.

"Sure you will," Kirk said. "Go ahead."

Charlie managed an awkward drop. He forgot to slap until almost the last minute, so that quite a thud accompanied the slap.

"Well, that's an improvement," Kirk said. "Like everything else, it takes practice. Once more."

This time was better. Kirk said, "That's it. Okay, Sam, show him a shoulder roll."

Ellis hit the mat, and was at once on his feet again, cleanly and easily.

"I don't want to do that," Charlie said.

"It's part of the course," Kirk said. "It's not hard. Look." He did a roll himself. "Try it."

"No. You were going to teach me to fight, not roll around on the floor."

"You have to learn to take falls without hurting yourself before we can do that. Sam, maybe we'd better demonstrate. A couple of easy throws."

"Sure," Ellis said. The two officers grappled, and Ellis, who was in much better shape than the Captain, let Kirk throw him. Then, as Kirk got to his feet, Ellis flipped him like a poker chip. Kirk rolled and bounced, glad of the exercise.

"See what I mean?" Kirk said.

"I guess so," Charlie said. "It doesn't look hard."

He moved in and grappled with Kirk, trying for the hold he had seen Ellis use. He was strong, but he had no leverage. Kirk took a counter-hold and threw him. It was not a hard throw, but Charlie again forgot to slap the mat. He jumped to his feet flaming mad, glaring at Kirk.

"*That* won't do," Ellis said, grinning. "You need a lot more falls, Charlie."

Charlie whirled toward him. In a low, intense voice, he said: "Don't laugh at me."

"Cool off, Charlie," Ellis said, chuckling openly now. "Half the trick is in not losing your temper."

"*Don't laugh at me!*" Charlie said. Ellis spread out his hands, but his grin did not quite go away.

Exactly one second later, there was a pop like the breaking of the world's largest light bulb. Ellis vanished.

Kirk stared stupefied at the spot where Ellis had been. Charlie, too, stood frozen for a moment. Then he began to move tentatively toward the door.

"Hold it," Kirk said. Charlie stopped, but he did not turn to face Kirk.

"He shouldn't have laughed at me," Charlie said. "That's not nice, to laugh at somebody. I was trying."

"Not very hard. Never mind that. What happened? What did you do to my officer?"

"He's gone," Charlie said sullenly.

"That's no answer."

"He's gone," Charlie said. "That's all I know. I didn't want to do it. He made me. He laughed at me."

And suppose Janice has to slap him? And ... there was the explosion of the *Antares* ... Kirk stepped quickly to the nearest wall intercom and flicked it on. Charlie turned at last to watch him. "Captain Kirk in the gym," Kirk said. "Two men from security here, on the double."

"What are you going to do with me?" Charlie said.

"I'm sending you to your quarters. And I want you to stay there."

"I won't let them touch me," Charlie said in a low voice. "I'll make them go away too."

"They won't hurt you."

Charlie did not answer, but he had the look of a caged animal just before it turns at last upon its trainer. The door opened and two security guards came in, phaser pistols holstered. They stopped and looked to Kirk.

"Go with them, Charlie. We'll talk about this later, when we've both cooled off. You owe me a long explanation." Kirk jerked his head toward Charlie. The guards stepped to him and took him by the arms.

Or, tried to. Actually, Kirk was sure that they never touched him. One of them simply staggered back, but the other was thrown violently against the wall, as though he had been caught in a sudden hurricane. He managed to hold his footing, however, and clawed for his sidearm.

"No!" Kirk shouted.

But the order was way too late. By the time the guard had his hand levelled at the boy, he no longer had a weapon to hold. It had vanished, just like Sam Ellis. Charlie stared at Kirk, his eyes narrowed and challenging.

"Charlie," Kirk said, "you're showing off. Go to your quarters."

"No."

"Go with the guards, or I'll pick you up and carry you there myself." He began to walk steadily forward. "That's your only choice, Charlie. Either do as I tell you, or send me away to wherever you sent the phaser, and Sam Ellis."

"Oh, all right," Charlie said, wilting. Kirk drew a deep breath. "But tell them to keep their hands to themselves."

"They won't hurt you. Not if you do as I say."

Kirk called a general council on the bridge at once, but Charlie moved faster: by the time Kirk's officers were all present, there wasn't a phaser to be found anywhere aboard ship. Charlie had made them all "go away." Kirk explained what had happened, briefly and grimly.

"Given this development," McCoy said, "it's clear Charlie wouldn't have needed any help from any putative Thasians. He could have magicked up all his needs by himself."

"Not necessarily," Spock said. "All we know is that he can make things vanish—not make them appear. I admit that that alone would have been a big help to him."

"What are the chances," Kirk said, "that he's a Thasian himself? Or at least, something really unprecedented in the way of an alien?"

"The chance is there," McCoy said, "but I'd be inclined to rule it out. Remember I checked him over. He's ostensibly human, down to his last blood type. Of course, I could have missed something, but he was hooked to the body-function panel, too; the machine would have rung sixteen different kinds of alarms at the slightest discrepancy."

"Well, he's inhumanly powerful, in any event," Spock said. "The probability is that he was responsible for the destruction of the *Antares*, too. Over an enormous distance—well beyond phaser range."

"Great," McCoy said. "Under the circumstances, how can we hope to keep him caged up?"

"It goes further than that, Bones," Kirk said. "We can't take him to Colony Five, either. Can you imagine what he'd do in an open, normal environment—in an undisciplined environment?"

Clearly, McCoy hadn't. Kirk got up and began to pace.

"Charlie is an adolescent boy—probably human, but totally inexperienced with other human beings. He's short-tempered because he wants so much and it can't come fast enough for him. He's full of adolescent aches. He wants to be one of us, to be loved, to be useful. But ... I remember when I was seventeen that I wished for the ability to remove the things and people that annoyed me, neatly and without fuss. It's a power fantasy most boys of that age have. Charlie doesn't have to wish. *He can do it.*

"In other words, in order to stay in existence, gentlemen, we'll have to make damn sure we don't annoy him. Otherwise—pop!"

"Annoyance is relative, Captain," Spock said. "It's all going to depend on how Charlie is feeling minute by minute. And because of his background, or lack of it, we have no ways to guess what little thing might annoy him next, no matter how carefully we try. He's the galaxy's most destructive weapon, and he's on a hair trigger."

"No," Kirk said. "He's not a weapon. He *has* a weapon. That's a difference we can use. Essentially, he's a child, a child in a man's body, trying to be a whole man. His trouble isn't malice. It's innocence."

"And here he is," McCoy said with false heartiness. Kirk swung his chair around to see Charlie approaching from the elevator, smiling cheerfully.

"Hi," said the galaxy's most destructive weapon.

"I thought I confined you to your quarters, Charlie."

"You did," Charlie said, the grin fading. "But I got tired of waiting around down there."

"Oh, all right. You're here. Maybe you can answer a few questions for us. Were you responsible for what happened to the *Antares*?"

"Why?"

"Because I want to know. Answer me, Charlie."

Breaths were held while Charlie thought it over. Finally, he said: "Yes. There was a warped baffle plate on the shielding of their Nerst generator. I made it go away. It would have given sooner or later anyhow."

"You could have told them that."

"What for?" Charlie said reasonably. "They weren't nice to me. They didn't like me. You saw them when they brought me aboard. They wanted to get rid of me. They don't any more."

"And what about us?" Kirk said.

"Oh, I need you. I have to get to Colony Five. But if you're not nice to me, I'll think of something else." The boy turned abruptly and left, for no visible reason.

McCoy wiped sweat off his forehead. "What a chance you took."

"We can't be walking on eggs every second," Kirk said. "If every act, every question might irritate him, we might as well pretend that none of them will. Otherwise we'll be utterly paralyzed."

"Captain," Spock said slowly, "do you suppose a force field might hold him? He's too smart to allow himself to be lured into a detention cell, but we just might rig up a field at his cabin door. All the lab circuitry runs through the main corridor on deck five, and we could use that. It's a long chance, but—"

"How long would the work take?" Kirk said.

"At a guess, seventy-two hours."

"It's going to be a long seventy-two hours, Mr. Spock. Get on it." Spock nodded and went out.

"Lieutenant Uhura, raise Colony Five for me. I want to speak directly to the Governor. Lieutenant Sulu, lay me a course away from Colony Five—not irrevocably, but enough to buy me some time. Bones—"

He was interrupted by the sound of a fat spark, and a choked scream of pain from Uhura. Her hands were in her lap, writhing together uncontrollably. McCoy leapt to her side, tried to press the clenched fingers apart.

"It's . . . all right," she said. "I think. Just a shock. But there's no reason for the board to be charged like that—"

"Probably a very good reason," Kirk said grimly. "Don't touch it until further orders. How does it look, Bones?"

"Superficial burns," McCoy said. "But who knows what it'll be next time?"

"I can tell you that," Sulu said. "I can't feed new co-ordinates into this panel. It operates, but it rejects the course change. We're locked on Colony Five."

"I'm in a hurry," Charlie's voice said. He was coming out of the elevator again, but he paused as he saw the naked fury on Kirk's face.

"I'm getting tired of this," Kirk said. "What about the transmitter?"

"You don't need all that subspace chatter," Charlie said, a little defensively. "If there's any trouble, I can take care of it myself. I'm learning fast."

"I don't want your help," Kirk said. "Charlie, for the moment there's nothing I can do to prevent your interference. But I'll tell you this: you're quite right, I don't like you. I don't like you at all. Now beat it."

"I'll go," Charlie said, quite coolly. "I don't mind if you don't like me now. You will pretty soon. I'm going to make you."

As he left, McCoy began to swear in a low whisper.

"Belay that, Bones, it won't help. Lieutenant Uhura, is it just outside communications that are shorted, or is the intercom out too?"

"Intercom looks good, Captain."

"All right, get me Yeoman Rand . . . Janice, I have a nasty one for you—maybe the nastiest you've ever been asked to do. I want you to lure Charlie into his cabin. . . . That's right. We'll be watching—but bear in mind that if you make him mad, there won't be much we can do to protect you. You can opt out if you want; it probably won't work anyhow."

"If it doesn't," Yeoman Rand's voice said, "it won't be because *I* didn't try it."

They watched, Spock's hand hovering over the key

that would activate the force field. At first, Janice was alone in Charlie's cabin, and the wait seemed very long. Finally, however, the door slid aside, and Charlie came into the field of the hidden camera, his expression a mixture of hope and suspicion.

"It was nice of you to come here," he said. "But I don't trust people any more. They're all so complicated, and full of hate."

"No, they're not," Janice said. "You just don't make enough allowance for how *they* feel. You have to give them time."

"Then . . . you do like me?"

"Yes, I like you. Enough to try to straighten you ou+ anyhow. Otherwise I wouldn't have asked to come here."

"That was very nice," Charlie said. "I can be nice, too. Look. I have something for you."

From behind his back, where it had already been visible to the camera, he produced the single pink rosebud he had been carrying and held it out. There had been no roses aboard ship, either; judging by that and the perfume, he could indeed make things appear as well as disappear. The omens did not look good.

"Pink *is* your favorite color, isn't it?" Charlie was saying. "The books say all girls like pink. Blue is for boys."

"It was . . . a nice thought, Charlie. But this isn't really the time for courting. I really need to talk to you."

"But you asked to come to my room. The books all say that means something important." He reached out, trying to touch her face. She moved instinctively away, trying to circle for the door, which was now on remote control, the switch for it under Spock's other hand; but she could not see where she was backing and was stopped by a chair.

"No. I said I only wanted to talk and that's what I meant."

"But I only wanted to be nice to you."

She got free of the chair somehow and resumed sidling. "That's a switch on Charlie's Law," she said.

"What do you mean? What's that?"

"Charlie's Law says everybody better be nice to Charlie, or else."

"That's not true!" Charlie said raggedly.

"Isn't it? Where's Sam Ellis, then?"

"I don't know where he is. He's just gone. Janice, I only *want* to be nice. They won't let me. None of you will. I can give you anything you want. Just tell me."

"All right," Janice said. "Then I think you had better let me go. That's what I want now."

"But you said..." The boy swallowed and tried again. "Janice, I ... love you."

"No you don't. You don't know what the word means."

"Then show me," he said, reaching for her.

Her back was to the door now, and Spock hit the switch. The boy's eyes widened as the door slid back, and then Janice was through it. He charged after her, and the other key closed.

The force field flared, and Charlie was flung back into the room. He stood there for a moment like a stabled stallion, nostrils flared, breathing heavily. Then he said:

"All right. All right, then."

He walked slowly forward. Kirk swung the camera to follow him. This time he went through the force field as though it did not exist. He advanced again on Janice.

"Why did you do that?" he said. "You won't even let me try. None of you. All right. From now on I'm not trying. I won't keep any of you but the ones I need. I don't need you."

There came the implosion sound again. Janice was gone. Around Kirk, the universe turned a dull, aching gray.

"Charlie," he said hoarsely. The intercom carried his voice to Charlie's cabin. He looked blindly toward the source.

"You too, Captain," he said. "What you did wasn't nice either. I'll keep you a while. The *Enterprise* isn't quite like the *Antares*. Running the *Antares* was easy.

But if you try to hurt me again, I'll make a lot of other people go away...I'm coming up to the bridge now."

"I can't stop you," Kirk said.

"I know you can't. Being a man isn't so much. I'm not a man and I can do anything. You can't. Maybe I'm the man and you're not."

Kirk cut out the circuit and looked at Spock. After a while the First Officer said:

"That was the last word, if ever I heard it."

"It's as close as I care to come to it, that's for sure. Did that field react at all, the second time?"

"No. He went through it as easily as a ray of light. Easier—I could have stopped a light ray if I'd known the frequency. There seems to be very little he can't do."

"Except run the ship—and get to Colony Five by himself."

"Small consolation."

They broke off as Charlie entered. He was walking very tall. Without a word to anyone, he went to the helmsman's chair and waved to Sulu to get out of it. After a brief glance at Kirk, Sulu got up obediently, and Charlie sat down and began to play with the controls. The ship lurched, very slightly, and he snatched his hands back.

"Show me what to do," he told Sulu.

"That would take thirty years of training."

"Don't argue with me. Just show me."

"Go ahead, show him," Kirk said. "Maybe he'll blow us up. Better than letting him loose on Colony Five—"

"Captain Kirk," Lieutenant Uhura broke in. "I'm getting something from outside; subspace channel F. Ship to ship, I think. But it's all on instruments; I can't hear it."

"There's nothing there," Charlie said, his voice rough. "Just leave it alone."

"Captain?"

"I am the captain," Charlie said. Yet somehow, Kirk had the sudden conviction that he was frightened. And somehow, equally inexplicably, he knew that the *Enterprise* had to get that call.

"Charlie," he said, "are you creating that message—or are you blocking one that's coming in?"

"It's my game, Mr. Kirk," Charlie said. "You have to find out. Like you said—that's how the game is played." He pushed himself out of the chair and said to Sulu, "You can have it now. I've locked on course for Colony Five again."

He could have done nothing of the sort in that brief period; not, at least, with his few brief stabs at the controls. Probably, his original lock still held unchanged. But either way, it was bad enough; Colony Five was now only twelve hours away.

But Charlie's hands were trembling visibly. Kirk said:

"All right, Charlie, that's the game—and the game is over. I don't think you can handle any more. I think you're at your limit and you can't take on one more thing. But you're going to have to. Me."

"I could have sent you away before," Charlie said. "Don't make me do it now."

"You don't dare. You've got my ship. I want it back. And I want my crew back whole, too—if I have to break your neck to do it."

"Don't push me," Charlie whispered. "*Don't push me.*"

At the next step forward, a sleet-storm of pain threw Kirk to the deck. He could not help crying out.

"I'm sorry," Charlie said, sweating. "I'm sorry—"

The subspace unit hummed loudly, suddenly, and then began to chatter in intelligible code. Uhura reached for the unscrambler.

"Stop that!" Charlie screamed, whirling. "I said, stop it!"

The pain stopped; Kirk was free. After a split-second's hesitation to make sure he was all there, he lunged to his feet. Spock and McCoy were also closing in, but Kirk was closer. He drew back a fist.

"Console is clear," Sulu's voice said behind him. "Helm answers."

Charlie dodged away from Kirk's threat, whimpering. He never had looked less like the captain of anything, even his own soul. Kirk held back his blow in wonder.

Pop!

Janice Rand was on the bridge, putting out both hands to steady herself. She was white-faced and shaken, but otherwise unharmed.

Pop!

"That was a hell of a fall, Jim," Sam Ellis' voice said. "Next time, take it a little—hey, what's all this?"

"Message is through," Lieutenant Uhura's voice said dispassionately. "Ship off our starboard bow. Identifies itself as from Thasus."

With a cry of animal panic, Charlie fell to the deck, drumming on it with both fists.

"Don't listen, don't listen!" he wailed. "No, no please! I can't live with them any more."

Kirk watched stolidly, not moving. The boy who had been bullying and manipulating them for so long was falling apart under his eyes.

"You're my friends. You *said* you were my friends. Remember—when I came aboard?" He looked up piteously at Kirk. "Take me home, to Colony Five. That's all I want . . . It's really all I want!"

"Captain," Spock said in an emotionless voice. "Something happening over here. Like a transporter materialization. Look."

Feeling like a man caught in a long fall of dominoes, Kirk jerked his eyes toward Spock. There was indeed something materializing on the bridge, through which Spock himself could now be seen only dimly. It was perhaps two-thirds as tall as a man, roughly oval, and fighting for solidity. It wavered and changed, and colors flowed through it. For a moment it looked like a gigantic human face; then, like nothing even remotely human; then, like a distorted view of a distant but gigantic building. It did not seem able to hold any state very long.

Then it spoke. The voice was deep and resonant. It came, not from the apparition, but from the subspace speaker; but like the apparition, it wavered, blurred, faded, blared, changed color, as if almost out of control.

"We are sorry for this trouble," it said. "We did not realize until too late that the human boy was gone from us. We searched a long time to find him, but space travel is a long-unused skill among us; we are saddened that his escape cost the lives of those aboard the first ship. We could not help them because they were exploded in this frame; but we have returned your people and your weapons to you, since they were only intact in the next frame. Now everything else is as it was. There is nothing to fear; we have him in control."

"No," Charlie said. He was weeping convulsively. Clambering to his knees, he grappled Kirk by a forearm. "I won't do it again. Please, I'll be nice. I won't ever do it again. I'm sorry about the *Antares,* I'm sorry. Please let me go with you, please!"

"Whee-oo," McCoy said gustily. "Talk about the marines landing—!"

"It's not that easy," Kirk said, looking steadily at the strange thing—a Thasian?—before him. "Charlie destroyed the other ship and will have to be punished for it. But thanks to you, all the other damage is repaired— and he is a human being. He belongs with his own people."

"You're out of your mind," McCoy said.

"Shut up, Bones. He's one of us. Rehabilitation might make him really one of us, reunite him to his own people. We owe him that, if he can be taught not to use his power."

"We gave him the power," the apparition said, "so that he could live. It cannot be taken back or forgotten. He will use it; he cannot help himself. He would destroy you and your kind, or you would be forced to destroy him to save yourselves. We alone offer him life."

"Not at all," Kirk said. "You offer him a prison— not even a half-life."

"We know that. But that damage was done long ago; we can do now only what little best is left. Since we are to blame, we must care for him. Come, Charles Evans."

"Don't let them!" Charlie gasped. "Don't let them take me! Captain—*Janice*! Don't you understand, I *can't even touch them*—"

The boy and the Thasian vanished, in utter silence. The only remaining sound was the dim, multifarious humming surround of the *Enterprise*.

And the sound of Janice Rand weeping, as a woman weeps for a lost son.

Dagger of the Mind

☆☆☆

Simon van Gelder came aboard the *Enterprise* from the Tantalus Penal Colony via transporter, inside a box addressed to the Bureau of Penology in Stockholm—a desperate measure, but not a particularly intelligent one, as was inevitable under the circumstances. He had hardly been aboard three minutes before Tristan Adams, the colony's director and chief medic, had alerted Captain Kirk to the escape ("a potentially violent case") and the search was on.

Nevertheless, in this short time van Gelder, who was six feet four and only in his early forties, was able to ambush a crewman, knock him out, and change clothes with him, acquiring a phaser pistol in the process. Thus disguised, he was able to make his way to the bridge, where he demanded asylum and managed to paralyze operations for three more minutes before being dropped from behind by one of Mr. Spock's famous nerve squeezes. He was then hauled off to be confined in sick bay, and that was that.

Or that should have been that. Standard operating procedure would have been to give the captive a routine medical check and then ship him by transporter back to Tantalus and the specialized therapeutic resources of Dr. Adams. Kirk, however, had long been an admirer of

23

Dr. Adams' rehabilitation concepts, and had been disappointed that ship's business had given him no excuse to visit the colony himself; now the irruption of this violent case seemed to offer an ideal opportunity. Besides, there was something about van Gelder himself that intrigued Kirk; in their brief encounter, he had not struck Kirk as a common criminal despite his desperation, and Kirk had not been aware that noncriminal psychiatric cases were ever sent to Tantalus. He went to visit the prisoner in the sick bay.

Dr. McCoy had him under both restraint and sedation while running body function tests. Asleep, his face was relaxed, childlike, vulnerable.

"I'm getting bursts of delta waves from the electroencephalograph," McCoy said, pointing to the body function panel. "Highly abnormal, but not schizophrenia, tissue damage, or any other condition I'm acquainted with. After I got him here, it took a triple dose of sedation to—"

He was interrupted by a sound from the bed, a strange combination of groan and snarl. The patient was coming back to consciousness, struggling against his bonds.

"The report said he was quite talkative," Kirk said.

"But not very informative. He'd claim one thing, seem to forget, then start to claim something else . . . and yet what little I could understand seemed to have the ring of truth to it. Too bad we won't have time to study him."

"So that's the system, is it?" the man on the bed said harshly, still struggling. "Take him back! Wash your hands of him! Let somebody else worry! Damn you—"

"What's your name?" Kirk said.

"My name . . . my name . . ." Suddenly, it seemed to Kirk that he was struggling not against the restraints, but against some kind of pain. "My name is . . . is Simon . . . Simon van Gelder."

He sank back and added almost quietly: "I don't suppose you've heard of me."

"Same name he gave before," McCoy said.

"Did I?" said van Gelder. "I'd forgotten. I was Director of ... of ... at the Tantalus Colony. Not a prisoner ... I was ... assistant. Graduate of ... of ..." His face contorted. "And then at ... I did graduate studies at ... studies at ..."

The harder the man tried to remember, the more pain he seemed to be in. "Never mind," Kirk said gently. "It's all right. We—"

"I know," van Gelder said through clenched teeth. "They erased it ... edited, adjusted ... subverted me! I won't ... I won't forget it! Won't go back there! Die first! Die, die!"

He had suddenly gone wild again, straining and shouting, his face a mask of unseeing passion. McCoy stepped close and there was the hiss of a spray hypo. The shouting died down to a mutter, then stopped altogether.

"Any guesses at all?" Kirk said.

"One point I don't have to guess at," McCoy said. "He doesn't want to go back to that—how did you describe it? 'More like a resort than a prison.' Evidently a cage is still a cage, no matter how you label it."

"Or else there's something drastically wrong down there," Kirk said. "Keep him secure, Bones. I'm going to do a little research."

By the time Kirk returned to the bridge, Spock was already removing a tape casette from the viewer. "I got this from our library, Captain," he said. "No doubt about it: our captive is Dr. van Gelder."

"Dr.—?"

"That's right. Assigned to Tantalus Colony six months ago as Dr. Adams' assistant. Not committed; assigned. A highly respected man in his field."

Kirk thought about it a moment, then turned to his Communications Officer. "Lieutenant Uhura, get me Dr. Adams on Tantalus ... Doctor? This is Captain Kirk of the *Enterprise*. Regarding your escapee—"

"Is Dr. van Gelder all right?" Adams' voice cut in with apparent concern. "And your people? No injuries? In the violent state he's in—"

"No harm to him or anyone, sir. But we thought you might be able to enlighten us about his condition. My medical officer is baffled."

"I'm not surprised. He'd been doing some experimental work, Captain. An experimental beam we'd hoped might rehabilitate incorrigibles. Dr. van Gelder felt he hadn't the moral right to expose another man to something he hadn't tried on his own person."

While Adams had been talking, McCoy had entered from the elevator and had crossed to the library-computer station, where he stood listening with Kirk and Spock. Now he caught Kirk's eye and made the immemorial throat-cutting gesture.

"I see," Kirk said into the microphone. "Please stand by a moment, Dr. Adams." Uhura broke contact, and Kirk swung to McCoy. "Explain."

"It doesn't quite ring true, Jim," the medico said. "I don't think whatever's wrong with this patient is something he did to himself. I think it was something that was done to him. I can't defend it, it's just an impression—but a strong one."

"That's not enough to go on," Kirk said, irritated in spite of himself. "You're not dealing with just any ordinary warden here, Bones. In the past twenty years, Adams has done more to revolutionize, to humanize, prisons and the treatment of prisoners than all the rest of humanity had done in forty centuries. I've been to penal colonies since they've begun following his methods. They're not 'cages' any more, they're clean, decent hospitals for sick minds. I'm not about to start throwing unsubstantiated charges against a man like that."

"Who said anything about charges?" McCoy said calmly. "Just ask questions. Propose an investigation. If something's really wrong, Adams will duck. Any harm in trying it?"

"I suppose not." Kirk nodded to Uhura, who closed the circuit again. "Dr. Adams? This is rather embarrassing. One of my officers has just reminded me that by strict interpretation of our starship regulations, I'm required to initiate an investigation of this so that a proper report—"

"No need to apologize, Captain Kirk," Adams' voice said. "In fact, I'd take it as a personal favor if you could beam down personally, look into it yourself. I'm sure you realize that I don't get too many visitors here. Oh—I would appreciate it if you could conduct the tour with a minimum staff. We're forced to limit outside contact as much as possible."

"I understand. I've visited rehab colonies before. Very well. *Enterprise* out . . . Satisfied, McCoy?"

"Temporarily," the medical officer said, unruffled.

"All right. We'll keep van Gelder here until I complete my investigation, anyway. Find me somebody in your department with psychiatric *and* penological experience—both in the same person, if possible."

"Helen Noel should do nicely. She's an M.D., but she's written several papers on rehab problems."

"Very good. We beam down in an hour."

Though there were plenty of women among the *Enterprise's* officers and crew, Helen Noel was a surprise to Kirk. She was young and almost uncomfortably pretty—and furthermore, though Kirk had seen her before, he had not then realized that she was part of the ship's complement. That had been back at the medical lab's Christmas party. He had had the impression then that she was simply a passenger, impressed as female passengers often were to be singled out for conversation by the Captain; and in fact, in the general atmosphere of Holiday he had taken certain small advantages of her impressionability . . . It now turned out that she was, and had then been, the newest addition to the ship's medical staff. Her expression as they met in the transporter room was demure, but he had the distinct impression that she was enjoying his discomfiture.

Tantalus was an eerie world, lifeless, ravaged, and torn by a bitter and blustery climate, its atmosphere mostly nitrogen slightly diluted by some of the noble gasses—a very bad place to try to stage an escape. In this it closely resembled all other penal colonies, enlightened or otherwise. Also as usual, the colony proper was all underground, its location marked on the surface only by a small superstructure containing a transporter room, an elevator head, and a few other service modules.

Dr. Tristan Adams met them in his office: a man in his mid-forties, with broad warm features, a suspicion of old freckles at the nose, and an almost aggressively friendly manner which seemed to promise firm handshakes, humor, an ounce of brandy at the right hour, and complete candor at all times. He hardly seemed to be old enough to have accumulated his massive reputation. The office reflected the man; it was personal, untidy without being littered, furnished with an eye to comfort and the satisfaction of someone perhaps as interested in primitive sculpture as in social medicine.

With him was a young woman, tall and handsome though slightly cadaverous, whom he introduced as "Lethe." There was something odd about her which Kirk could not quite fathom: perhaps a slight lack of normal human spontaneity in both manner and voice. As if expecting just such a reaction, Adams went on:

"Lethe came to us for rehabilitation, and ended up staying on as a therapist. And a very good one."

"I love my work," the girl said, in a flat voice.

With a glance at Adams for permission, Kirk said: "And before you came here?"

"I was another person," Lethe said. "Malignant, hateful."

"May I ask what crime you committed?"

"I don't know," Lethe said. "It doesn't matter. That person no longer exists."

"Part of our treatment, Captain, is to bury the past," Adams said. "If the patient can come to terms with his memories, all well and good. But if they're unbearable, why carry them at all? Sufficient unto the day are the burdens thereof. Shall we begin the tour?"

"I'm afraid we haven't time for a complete tour,"

Kirk said. "Under the circumstances, I'd primarily like to see the apparatus or experiment that injured Dr. van Gelder. That, after all, is the whole point of our inquiry."

"Yes, quite. One doesn't enjoy talking about failures, but still, negative evidence is also important. If you'll just follow me—"

"One minute," Kirk said, pulling his communicator out of his hip pocket. "I'd best check in with the ship. If you'll pardon me a moment—?"

Adams nodded and Kirk stepped to one side, partly turning his back. In a moment, Spock's voice was saying softly:

"Van Gelder's no better, but Dr. McCoy has pulled a few additional bits and pieces out of his memory. They don't seem to change the situation much. He insists that Adams is malignant, the machine is dangerous. No details."

"All right. I'll check in with you at four-hour intervals. Thus far everything here seems open and aboveboard. Out."

"Ready, Captain?" Adams said pleasantly. "Good. This way, please."

The chamber in which van Gelder had allegedly undergone his mysterious and shattering conversion looked to Kirk's unsophisticated eye exactly like any other treatment room, perhaps most closely resembling a radiology theater. There was a patient on the table as Kirk, Adams, and Helen entered, seemingly unconscious; and from a small, complex device hanging from the ceiling, a narrow, monochromatic beam of light like a laser beam was fixed on the patient's forehead. Near the door, a uniformed therapist stood at a small control panel, unshielded; evidently, the radiation, whatever it was, was not dangerous at even this moderate distance. It all looked quite unalarming.

"This is the device," Adams said softly. "A neural potentiator, or damper. The two terms sound opposite to each other but actually both describe the same effect:

an induced increase in neural conductivity, which greatly increases the number of cross-connections in the brain. At a certain point, as we predicted from information theory, increased connectivity actually results in the disappearance of information. We thought it would help the patient to cope better with his most troublesome thoughts and desires. But the effects are only temporary; so, I doubt that it'll be anything like as useful as we'd hoped it would be."

"Hmm," Kirk said. "Then if it's not particularly useful—"

"Why do we use it?" Adams smiled ruefully. "Hope, that's all, Captain. Perhaps we can still get some good out of it, in calming violent cases. But strictly as a palliative."

"Like tranquilizing drugs," Helen Noel suggested. "They do nothing permanent. And to continually be feeding drugs into a man's bloodstream just to keep him under control . . ."

Adams nodded vigorously. "Exactly my point, Doctor."

He turned toward the door, but Kirk was still eyeing the patient on the table. He swung suddenly on the uniformed therapist and said, "How does it operate?"

"Simply enough, it's nonselective," the therapist said. "On and off, and a potentiometer for intensity. We used to try to match the output to the patient's resting delta rhythms, but we found that wasn't critical. The brain seems to do its own monitoring, with some help from outside suggestion. For that, of course, you have to know the patient pretty well; you can't just put him on the table and expect the machine to process him like a computer tape."

"And we shouldn't be talking so much in his presence, for that very reason," Adams said, a faint trace of annoyance in his voice for the first time. "Better if further explanations waited until we're back in the office."

"I'd better ask my questions while they're fresh," Kirk said.

"The Captain," Helen said to Adams, "is an impulsive man."

Adams smiled. "He reminds me a little of the ancient skeptic who demanded to be taught all the world's wisdom while he stood on one foot."

"I simply want to be sure," Kirk said stonily, "that this is in fact where Dr. van Gelder's injury occurred."

"Yes," Adams said, "and it was his own fault, if you must know. I dislike maligning a colleague, but the fact is that Simon is a stubborn man. He could have sat in here for a year with the beam adjusted to this intensity, or even higher. Or if there simply had been someone standing at the panel to cut the power when trouble began. But he tried it alone, at full amplitude. Naturally, it hurt him. Even water can poison a man, in sufficient volume."

"Careless of him," Kirk said, still without expression. "All right, Dr. Adams, let's see the rest."

"Very well. I'd like to have you meet some of our successes, too."

"Lead on."

In the quarters which Adams' staff had assigned him for the night, Kirk called the *Enterprise,* but there was still nothing essentially new. McCoy was still trying to get past the scars in van Gelder's memory, but nothing he had uncovered yet seemed contributory. Van Gelder was exhausted; toward the end, he would say nothing but, "He empties us . . . and then fills us with himself. I ran away before he could fill me. It is so lonely to be empty . . ."

Meaningless; yet somehow it added up to something in Kirk's mind. After a while, he went quietly out into the corridor and padded next door to Helen Noel's room.

"Well!" she said, at the door. "What's this, Captain? Do you think it's Christmas again?"

"Ship's business," Kirk said. "Let me in before somebody spots me. Orders."

She moved aside, hesitantly, and he shut the door behind himself.

"Thanks. Now then, Doctor: What did you think of the inmates we saw this afternoon?"

"Why . . . I was impressed, on the whole. They seemed happy, or at least well-adjusted, making progress—"

"And a bit blank?"

"They weren't normal. I didn't expect them to be."

"All right. I'd like to look at that treatment room again. I'll need you; you must have comprehended far more of the theory than I did."

"Why not ask Dr. Adams?" she said stiffly. "He's the only expert on the subject here."

"And if he's lying about anything, he'll continue to lie and I'll learn nothing. The only way I can be sure is to see the machine work. I'll need an operator; you're the only choice."

"Well . . . all right."

They found the treatment room without difficulty. There was nobody about. Quickly Kirk pointed out the controls the therapist had identified for him, then took up the position that had been occupied by the patient then. He looked ruefully up at the device on the ceiling.

"I'm expecting you to be able to tell if that thing is doing me any harm," he said. "Adams says it's safe; that's what I want to know. Try minimum output; only a second or two."

Nothing happened.

"Well? Any time you're ready."

"I've already given you two seconds."

"Hmm. Nothing happened at all."

"Yes, something did. You were frowning; then your face went blank. When I cut the power, the frown came back."

"I didn't notice a thing. Try it again."

"How do you feel now?"

"Somewhat . . . uh, nothing definite. Just waiting. I thought we were going to try again."

"We did," Helen said. "It looks as though your mind

goes so completely blank that you don't even feel the passage of time."

"Well, well," Kirk said drily. "Remarkably effective for a device Adams said he was thinking of abandoning. The technician mentioned that suggestion was involved. Try one—something harmless, please. You know, when we finally get through this, I hope we can raid a kitchen somewhere."

"It works," Helen said in a strained voice. "I gave you two seconds at low intensity and said, 'You're hungry.' And now you are."

"I didn't hear a thing. Let's give it one more try. I don't want to leave any doubt about it."

"Quite right," Adams' voice said. Kirk sat bolt upright, to find himself staring squarely into the business end of a phaser pistol. The therapist was there too, another gun held unwaveringly on Helen.

"Prisons and mental hospitals," Adams went on, smiling, almost tolerantly, "monitor every conversation, every sound—or else they don't last long. So I'm able to satisfy your curiosity, Captain. We'll give you a proper demonstration."

He stepped to the control panel and turned the potentiometer knob. Kirk never saw him hit the on-off button. The room simply vanished in a wave of intolerable pain.

As before, there was no time lapse at all; he only found himself on his feet, handing his phaser to Adams. At the same time, he knew what the pain was: it was love for Helen, and the pain of loneliness, of being without her. She was gone; all he had was the memory of having carried her to her cabin that Christmas, of her protests, of his lies that had turned into truth. Curiously, the memories seemed somewhat colorless, one-dimensional, the voices in them, monotonous; but the longing and the loneliness were real. To assuage it, he would lie, cheat, steal, give up his ship, his reputation ... He cried out.

"She's not here," Adams said, passing Kirk's phaser to the therapist. "I'll send her back in a while and then things will be better. But first, it's time to call your vessel. It's important that they know all is well. Then perhaps we can see Dr. Noel."

Through a renewed stab of pain, Kirk got out his communicator and snapped it open. "Captain . . . to *Enterprise*," he said. He found it very difficult to speak; the message did not seem to be important.

"Enterprise here, Captain," Spock's voice said.

"All is well, Mr. Spock. I'm still with Dr. Adams."

"You sound tired, Captain. No problems?"

"None at all, Mr. Spock. My next call will be in six hours. Kirk out."

He started to pocket the communicator, but Adams held out his hand.

"And that, too, Captain."

Kirk hesitated. Adams reached for the control panel. The pain came back, redoubled, tripled, quadrupled; and now, at last, there came a real and blessed unconsciousness.

He awoke to the murmur of a feminine voice, and the feeling of a damp cloth being smoothed across his forehead. He opened his eyes. He was on his bed in the quarters on Tantalus; he felt as though he had been thrown there. A hand obscured his vision and he felt the cloth again. Helen's voice said:

"Captain . . . Captain. They've taken you out of the treatment room. You're in your own quarters now. Wake up, please, please!"

"Helen," he said. Automatically, he reached for her, but he was very weak; she pushed him back without effort.

"Try to remember. He put all that in your mind. Adams took the controls away from me—do you remember the pain? And then his voice, telling you you love me—"

He lifted himself on one elbow. The pain was there

all right, and the desire. He fought them both, sweating.

"Yes ... I think so," he said. Another wave of pain. "His machine's not perfect. I remember ... some of it."

"Good. Let me wet this rag again."

As she moved away, Kirk forced himself to his feet, stood dizzily for a moment, and then lurched forward to try the door. Locked, of course. In here, he and Helen were supposed to consolidate the impressed love, make it real ... and forget the *Enterprise*. Not bloody likely! Looking around, he spotted an air-conditioning grille.

Helen came back, and he beckoned to her, holding his finger to his lips. She followed him curiously. He tested the grille; it gave slightly. Throwing all his back muscles into it, he bent it outward. At the second try, it came free in his hand with a slight shearing sound. He knelt and poked his head into the opening.

The tunnel beyond was not only a duct; it was a crawl-space, intended also for servicing power lines. It could be crawled through easily, at least, as far as he could see down it. He tried it, but his shoulders were too bulky.

He stood up and held out his arms to the girl. She shrank back, but he jerked his head urgently, hoping that there was nothing in his expression which suggested passion. After a moment's more hesitation, she stepped against him.

"He may be watching as well as listening," Kirk whispered. "I'm just hoping he's focused on the bed, in that case. But that tunnel has to connect with a whole complex of others. It probably leads eventually to their power supply. If you can get through it, you can black out the whole place—and cut off their sensors, so Spock could beam us down some help without being caught at it. Game to try?"

"Of course."

"Don't touch any of those power lines. It'll be a bad squeeze."

"Better than Adams' treatment room."

"Good girl."

He looked down at her. The pain was powerful, reinforced by memory and danger, and her eyes were half-closed, her mouth willing. Somehow, all the same, he managed to break away. Dropping to her knees, she squirmed inside the tunnel and vanished, and Kirk began to replace the grille.

It was bent too badly to snap it back into place; he could only force it into reasonable shape and hope that nobody would notice that it wasn't fastened. He was on his feet and pocketing the sheared rivet heads when he heard the tumblers of the door lock clicking. He swung around just in time to see the therapist enter, holding an old-style phaser pistol. The man looked around incuriously.

"Where's the girl?" he said.

"Another of you zombies took her away. If you've hurt her, I'll kill you. Time for another 'treatment'?" He took a step closer, crouching. The pistol snapped up.

"Stand back! Cross in front of me and turn right in the corridor. I won't hesitate to shoot."

"That would be tough to explain to your boss. Oh, all right, I'm going."

Adams was waiting; he gestured curtly toward the table.

"What's the idea?" Kirk said. "I'm co-operating, aren't I?"

"If you were, you wouldn't have asked," Adams said. "However, I've no intention of explaining myself to you, Captain. Lie down. Good. Now."

The potentiator beam stabbed down at Kirk's head. He fought it, feeling the emptiness increase. This time, at least, he was aware of time passing, though he seemed to be accomplishing nothing else. His very will was draining away, as though somebody had opened a petcock on his skull.

"You believe in me completely," Adams said. "You believe in me. You trust me. The thought of distrusting me is intensely painful. You believe."

"I believe," Kirk said. To do anything else was agony.

"I believe in you. I trust you, I trust you! Stop, stop!"

Adams shut off the controls. The pain diminished slightly, but it was far from gone.

"I give you credit," Adams said thoughtfully. "Van Gelder was sobbing on his knees by now, and he had a strong will. I'm glad I've had a pair like you; I've learned a great deal."

"But . . . what . . . purpose? Your reputation . . . your . . . work . . ."

"So you can still ask questions? Remarkable. Never mind. I'm tired of doing things for others, that's all. I want a very comfortable old age, on my terms—and I am a most selective man. And you'll help me."

"Of course . . . but so unnecessary . . . just trust . . ."

"Trust you? Naturally. Or, trust mankind to reward me? All they've given me thus far is Tantalus. It's not enough. I know how their minds work. Nobody better."

There was the sound of the door, and then Kirk could see the woman therapist, Lethe. She said:

"Dr. Noel's gone. Nobody took her out. She just vanished."

Adams swung back to the panel and hit the switch. The beam came on, at full amplitude. Kirk's brainpan seemed to empty as if it had been dumped down a drain.

"Where is she?"

"I . . . don't know . . ."

The pain increased. "Where is she? Answer!"

There was no possibility of answering. He simply did not know, and the pain blocked any other answer but the specific one being demanded. As if realizing this, Adams backed the beam down a little.

"Where did you send her? With what instructions? *Answer!*"

The pain soared, almost to ecstasy—and at the same instant, all the lights went out but a dim safe light in the ceiling. Kirk did not have to stop to think what might have happened. Enraged by agony, he acted on reflex and training. A moment later, the therapist was sprawled on the floor and he had Lethe and Adams covered with the old-style phaser.

"No time for you now," he said. Setting the phaser to "stun," he pulled the trigger. Then he was out in the corridor, a solid mass of desire, loneliness, and fright. He had to get to Helen; there was nothing else in his mind at all, except a white line of pain at having betrayed someone he had been told to trust.

Dull-eyed, frightened patients milled about him as he pushed toward the center of the complex, searching for the power room. He shoved them out of the way. The search was like an endless nightmare. Then, somehow, he was with Helen, and they were kissing.

It did not seem to help. He pulled her closer. She yielded, but without any real enthusiasm. A moment later, there was a familiar hum behind him: the sound of a transporter materialization. Then Spock's voice said:

"Captain Kirk—what on—"

Helen broke free. "It's not his fault. Quick, Jim, where's Adams?"

"Above," Kirk said dully. "In the treatment room. Helen—"

"Later, Jim. We've got to hurry."

They found Adams sprawled across the table. The machine was still on. Lethe stood impassively beside the controls; as they entered, backed by a full force of security guards from the ship, she snapped them off.

McCoy appeared from somewhere and bent over Adams. Then he straightened.

"Dead."

"I don't understand," Helen said. "The machine wasn't on high enough to kill. I don't think it could kill."

"He was alone," Lethe said stonily. "That was enough. I did not speak to him."

Kirk felt his ringing skull. "I think I see."

"I can't say that I do, Jim," McCoy said. "A man has to die of something."

"He died of loneliness," Lethe said. "It's quite enough. I know."

"What do we do now, Captain?" Spock said.

"I don't know... let me see... get van Gelder down here and repair him, I guess. He'll have to take charge. And then... he'll have to decondition me. Helen, I don't want that, I want nothing less in the world; but—"

"I don't want it either," she said softly. "So we'll both have to go through it. It was nice while it lasted, Jim—awful, but nice."

"It's still hard to believe," McCoy said, much later, "that a man could die of loneliness."

"No," Kirk said. He was quite all right now; quite all right. Helen was nothing to him but another female doctor. But—

"No," he said, "it's not hard to believe at all."

The Unreal McCoy

☆☆

The crater campsite—or the Bierce campsite, as the records called it—on Regulus VIII was the crumbling remains of what might once have been a nested temple, surrounded now by archeological digs, several sheds, and a tumble of tools, tarpaulins, and battered artifacts. Outside the crater proper, the planet was largely barren except for patches of low, thorny vegetation, all the way in any direction to wherever the next crater might be— there were plenty of those, but there'd been no time to investigate them, beyond noting that they had all been inhabited once, unknown millennia ago. There was nothing uncommon about that; the galaxy was strewn with ruins about which nobody knew anything, there were a hundred such planets for every archeologist who could even dream of scratching such a surface. Bierce had just been lucky—fantastically lucky.

All the same, Regulus VIII made Kirk—Capt. James Kirk of the starship *Enterprise*, who had seen more planets than most men knew existed—feel faintly edgy. The *Enterprise* had landed here in conformity to the book; to be specific, to that part of the book which said that research personnel on alien planets must have their health certified by a starship's surgeon at one-year intervals. The *Enterprise* had been in Bierce's vicinity at the statutory time, and Ship's Surgeon McCoy had come down by transporter from the orbiting *Enterprise* to do the job. Utterly, completely routine, except for the fact that McCoy had mentioned that Bierce's wife Nancy had been a serious interest of McCoy's, pre-Bierce, well over ten years ago. And after all, what could be more commonplace than that?

Then Nancy came out of the temple—if that is what it was—to meet them.

There were only three of them: McCoy and a crewman, Darnell, out of duty, and Kirk, out of curiosity. She came forward with outstretched hands, and after a moment's hesitation, McCoy took them. "Leonard!" she said. "Let me look at you."

"Nancy," McCoy said. "You . . . you haven't aged a year."

Kirk restrained himself from smiling. Nancy Bierce was handsome, but nothing extraordinary: a strongly built woman of about forty, moderately graceful, her hair tinged with gray. It wasn't easy to believe that the hard-bitten medico could have been so smitten, even at thirty or less, as to be unable to see the signs of aging now. Still, she did have a sweet smile.

"This is the Captain of the *Enterprise,* Jim Kirk," McCoy said. "And this is Crewman Darnell."

Nancy turned her smile on the Captain, and then on the crewman. Darnell's reaction was astonishing. His jaw swung open; he was frankly staring. Kirk would have kicked him had he been within reach.

"Come in, come in," she was saying. "We may have to wait a little for Bob; once he starts digging, he forgets time. We've made up some quarters in what seems to have been an old altar chamber—not luxurious, but lots of room. Come on in, Plum."

She ducked inside the low, crumbling stone door.

"Plum?" Kirk said.

"An old pet name," McCoy said, embarrassed. He followed her. Embarrassed himself at his own gaucherie, Kirk swung on the crewman.

"Just what are you goggling at, Mister?"

"Sorry, sir," Darnell said stiffly. "She reminds me of somebody, is all. A girl I knew once on Wrigley's Planet. That is—"

"That's enough," Kirk said drily. "The next thought of that kind you have will probably be in solitary. Maybe you'd better wait outside."

"Yessir. Thanks." Darnell seemed genuinely grateful. "I'll explore a little, if that suits you, Captain."

"Do that. Just stay within call."

Commonplace; Darnell hadn't seen a strange woman since his last landfall. But most peculiar, too.

Bierce did not arrive, and after apologies, Nancy left again to look for him, leaving Kirk and McCoy to examine the stone room, trying not to speak to each other. Kirk could not decide whether he would rather be back on board the *Enterprise*, or just plain dead; his diplomacy had not failed him this badly in he could not think how many years.

Luckily, Bierce showed up before Kirk had to decide whether to run or suicide. He was an unusually tall man, all knuckles, knees, and cheekbones, wearing faded coveralls. Slightly taller than McCoy, his face was as craggy as his body; the glint in the eyes, Kirk thought, was somehow both intelligent and rather bitter. But then, Kirk had never pretended to understand the academic type.

"Dr. Bierce," he said, "I'm Captain Kirk, and this is Ship's Surgeon—"

"I know who you are," Bierce broke in, in a voice with the blaring rasp of a busy signal. "We don't need you here. If you'll just refill us on aspirin, salt tablets, and the like, you needn't trouble yourselves further."

"Sorry, but the law requires an annual checkup," Kirk said. "If you'll co-operate, I'm sure Dr. McCoy will be as quick as possible." McCoy, in fact, already had his instruments out.

"McCoy?" Bierce said. "I've heard that name . . . Ah, yes, Nancy used to talk about you."

"Hands out from your sides, please, and breathe evenly . . . Yes, didn't she mention I'd arrived?"

After the slightest of pauses, Bierce said, "You've . . . seen Nancy?"

"She was here when we arrived," Kirk said. "She went to look for you."

"Oh. Quite so. I'm pleased, of course, that she can meet an old friend, have a chance of some company. I enjoy solitude, but it's difficult for a woman sometimes."

"I understand," Kirk said, but he was none too sure he did. The sudden attempt at cordiality rang false, somehow, after the preceding hostility. At least *that* had sounded genuine.

McCoy had finished his checkup with the tricorder and produced a tongue depressor with a small flourish. "She hasn't changed a bit," he said. "Open your mouth, please."

Reluctantly, Bierce complied. At the same instant, the air was split by a full-throated shriek of horror. For an insane moment Kirk had the impression that the sound had issued from Bierce's mouth. Then another scream ripped the silence, and Kirk realized that it was, of course, a female voice.

They all three bolted out the door. In the open, Kirk and McCoy outdistanced Bierce quickly; for all his outdoor life, he was not a good runner. But they hadn't far to go. Just beyond the rim of the crater, Nancy, both fists to her mouth, was standing over the body of Darnell.

As they came pounding up she moved toward McCoy, but he ignored her and dropped beside the body. It was lying on its face. After checking the pulse, McCoy gently turned the head to one side, grunted, and then turned the body over completely.

It was clear even to Kirk that the crewman was

dead. His face was covered with small ringlike red blotches, slowly fading. "What hit him?" Kirk said tensely.

"Don't know. Petachiae a little like vacuum mottling, or maybe some sort of immunological—hullo, what's this?"

Bierce came panting up as McCoy slowly forced open one of Darnell's fists. In it was a twisted, scabrous-looking object of no particular color, like a mummified parsnip. It looked also as though part of it had been bitten away. Now *that* was incredible. Kirk swung on Nancy.

"What happened?" he said tersely.

"Don't snap at my wife, Captain," Bierce said in his busy-signal voice. "Plainly it's not her fault!"

"One of my men is dead. I accuse nobody, but Mrs. Bierce is the only witness."

McCoy rose and said to Nancy, gently: "Just tell us what you saw, Nancy. Take your time."

"I was just . . ." she said, and then had to stop and swallow, as if fighting for control. "I couldn't find Bob, and I'd . . . I'd just started back when I saw your crewman. He had that borgia root in his hand and he was smelling it. I was just going to call out to him when— he bit into it. I had no idea he was going to—and then his face twisted and he fell—"

She broke off and buried her face in her hands. McCoy took her gently by one shoulder. Kirk, feeling no obligation to add one bedside manner more, said evenly: "How'd you know what the root was if you'd just come within calling distance?"

"This cross-examination—" Bierce grated.

"Bob, please. I didn't know, of course. Not until I saw it now. But it's dangerous to handle any plant on a new world."

Certainly true. Equally certainly, it would have been no news to Darnell. His face impassive, Kirk told McCoy: "Pack up, Bones. We can resume the physicals tomorrow."

"I'm sure that won't be necessary," Bierce said. "If you'll just disembark our supplies, Captain—"

"It's not going to be that easy, Dr. Bierce," Kirk said. He snapped open his communicator. "Kirk to Transporter Room. Lock and beam: two transportees and a corpse."

The autopsied body of Darnell lay on a table in the sick bay, unrecognizable now even by his mother, if so veteran a spaceman had ever had one. Kirk, standing near a communicator panel, watched with a faint physical uneasiness as McCoy lowered Darnell's brain into a shallow bowl and then turned and washed his hands until they were paper-white. Kirk had seen corpses in every conceivable state of distortion and age in one battle and another, but this clinical bloodiness was not within his experience.

"I can't rule poison out entirely," McCoy said, in a matter-of-fact voice. "Some of the best-known act just as fast and leave just as little trace: botulinus, for example. But there's no trace of any woody substance in his stomach or even between his teeth. All I can say for sure is that he's got massive capillary damage—which could be due to almost anything, even shock—and those marks on his face."

McCoy covered the ruined body. "I'll be running some blood chemistry tests, but I'd like to know what I'm testing for. I'd also like to know what symptoms that 'borgia root' is *supposed* to produce. Until then, Jim, I'm really rather in the dark."

"Spock's running a library search on the plant," Kirk said. "It shouldn't take him long. But I must confess that what you've said thus far doesn't completely surprise me. Darnell was too old a hand to bite into any old thing he happened to pick up."

"Then what's left? Nancy? Jim, I'm not quite trusting my own eyes lately, but Nancy didn't use to be capable of murder—certainly not of an utter stranger, to boot!"

"It's not only people who kill—hold it, here's the report. Go ahead, Mr. Spock."

"We have nothing on the borgia root but what the Bierces themselves reported in their project request six years ago," Spock's precise voice said. "There they call it an aconite resembling the *Lilium* family. Said to contain some twenty to fifty different alkaloids, none then identifiable specifically with the equipment to hand. The raw root is poisonous to mice. No mention of any human symptoms. Except . . ."

"Except what?" McCoy snapped.

"Well, Dr. McCoy, this isn't a symptom. The report adds that the root has a pleasant perfume, bland but edible-smelling, rather like tapioca. And that's all there is."

"Thanks." Kirk switched off. "Bones, I can't see Darnell having been driven irresistibly to bite into an unknown plant because it smelled like tapioca. He wouldn't have bitten into something that smelled like a brandied peach unless he'd known its pedigree. He was a seasoned hand."

McCoy spread his hands expressively. "You knew your man, Jim—but where does that leave us? The symptoms do vaguely resemble aconite poisoning. Beyond that, we're nowhere."

"Not quite," Kirk said. "We still have to check on the Bierces, I'm afraid, Bones. And for that I'm still going to need your help."

McCoy turned his back and resumed washing his hands. "You'll get it," he said; but his voice was very cold.

Kirk's method of checking on the Bierces was simple but drastic: he ordered them both on board the ship. Bierce raged.

"If you think you can beam down here, bully us, interfere with my work—considering the inescapable fact that you are a trespasser on my planet—"

"Your complaint is noted," Kirk said. "I apologize for the inconvenience. But it's also an inescapable fact that something we don't understand killed one of our men. It could very well be a danger to you, too."

"We've been here almost five years. If there was something hostile here we'd know about it by now, wouldn't we?"

"Not necessarily," Kirk said. "Two people can't know all the ins and outs of a whole planet, not even in five years—or a lifetime. In any event, one of the missions of the *Enterprise* is to protect human life in places like this. Under the circumstances, I'm going to have to be arbitrary and declare the argument closed."

It was shortly after they came aboard that McCoy forwarded his reports on the analyses of Darnell's body. "It was shock, all right," he told Kirk grimly by vid-screen. "But shock of a most peculiar sort. His blood electrolytes were completely deranged: massive salt depletion, hell—there isn't a microgram of salt in his whole body. Not in the blood, the tears, the organs, not anywhere. I can't even begin to guess how that could have happened at all, let alone all at once."

"What about the mottling on his face?"

"Broken capillaries. There are such marks all over the body. They're normal under the circumstances—except that I can't explain why they should be most marked on the face, or why the mottling should be ring-shaped. Clearly, though, he wasn't poisoned."

"Then the bitten plant," Kirk said equally grimly, "was a plant—in the criminal, not the botanical sense. A blind. That implies intelligence. I can't say I like that any better."

"Nor I," McCoy said. His eyes were averted.

"All right. That means we'll have to waste no time grilling the Bierces. I'll take it on. Bones, this has been a tremendous strain on you, I know, and you've been without sleep for two days. Better take a couple of tranquilizers and doss down."

"I'm all right."

"Orders," Kirk said. He turned off the screen and set off for the quarters he had assigned the Bierces.

But there was only one Bierce there. Nancy was missing.

"I expect she's gone below," Bierce said indifferently. "I'd go myself if I could get access to your Transporter for ten seconds. We didn't ask to be imprisoned up here."

"Darnell didn't ask to be killed, either. Your wife may be in serious danger. I must say, you seem singularly unworried."

"She's in no danger. This menace is all in your imagination."

"I suppose the body is imaginary, too?"

Bierce shrugged. "Nobody knows what could have killed him. For all I know, you brought your own menace with you."

There was nothing further to be got out of him. Exasperated, Kirk went back to the bridge and ordered a general search. The results were all negative—including the report from the Transporter Room, which insisted that nobody had used its facilities since the party had returned to the ship from the camp.

But the search, though it did not find Nancy, found something else: Crewman Barnhart, dead on Deck Twelve. The marks on his body were the same as those on Darnell's.

Baffled and furious, Kirk called McCoy. "I'm sorry to bust in on your sleep, Bones, but this has gone far enough. I want Bierce checked out under pentathol."

"Um," McCoy said. His voice sounded fuzzy, as though he had still not quite recovered from his tranquilizer dose. "Pentathol. Truth dope. Narcosynthesis. Um. Takes time. What about the patient's civil rights?"

"He can file a complaint if he wants. Go and get him ready."

An hour later, Bierce was lying on his bunk in half-trance. Kirk bent over him tensely; McCoy and Spock hovered in the background.

"Where's your wife?"

"Don't know . . . Poor Nancy, I loved her . . . The last of its kind . . ."

"Explain, please."

"The passenger pigeon . . . the buffalo . . ." Bierce groaned. "I feel strange."

Kirk beckoned to McCoy, who checked Bierce's pulse and looked under his eyelids. "He's all right," he said. "The transfer of questioner, from me to you, upset him. He's recovering."

"What about buffalo?" Kirk said, feeling absurd.

"Millions of them . . . prairies black with them. One single herd that covered three states. When they moved . . . like thunder. All gone now. Like the creatures here."

"Here? You mean down on the planet?"

"On the planet. Their temples . . . great poetry . . . Millions of them once, and now only one left. Nancy understood."

"Always the past tense," Spock's voice murmured.

"Where is Nancy? Where is she *now?*"

"Dead. Buried up on the hill. It killed her."

"Buried! But—how long ago was this, anyhow?"

"A year . . ." Bierce said. "Or was it two? I don't know. So confusing, Nancy and not Nancy. They needed salt, you see. When it ran out, they died . . . all but one."

The implication stunned Kirk. It was Spock who put the question.

"Is this creature masquerading as your wife?"

"Not a masquerade," Bierce droned. "It can *be* Nancy."

"Or anybody else?"

"Anybody. When it killed Nancy, I almost destroyed it. But I couldn't. It was the last."

The repetition was becoming more irritating every minute. Kirk said stonily: "Is that the only reason, Bierce? Tell me this: When it's with you, is it always Nancy?"

Bierce writhed. There was no answer. McCoy came forward again.

"I wouldn't press that one if I were you, Jim," he said. "You can get the answer if you need it, but not without endangering the patient."

"I don't need any better answer," Kirk said. "So we've intruded here into a little private heaven. The thing can be wife, lover, best friend, idol, slave, wise man, fool—anybody. A great life, having everyone in the universe at your beck and call—and you win all the arguments."

"A one-way road to paranoia," Spock said. Kirk swung back to the drugged man.

"Then can you recognize the creature—no matter what form it takes?"

"Yes . . ."

"Will you help us?"

"No."

Kirk had expected no more. He gestured to McCoy. "I've got to go organize a search. Break down that resistance, Bones, I don't care how you do it or how much you endanger Bierce. In his present state of mind he's as big a danger to us as his 'wife.' Spock, back him up, and be ready to shoot if he should turn violent."

He stalked out. On the bridge, he called a General Quarters Three; that would put pairs of armed men in every corridor, on every deck. "Every man inspect his mate closely," he told the intercom. "There's one extra person aboard, masquerading as one of us. Lieutenant Uhura, make television rounds of all posts and stations. If you see any person twice in different places, sound the alarm. Got it?"

A sound behind him made him swing around. It was Spock. His clothes were torn, and he was breathing heavily.

"Spock! I thought I told you—what happened?"

"It was McCoy," Spock said shakily. "Or rather, it wasn't McCoy. You were barely out of the cabin when it grabbed me. I got away, but it's got my sidearm. No telling where it's off to now."

"McCoy! I *thought* he seemed a little reluctant about

the pentathol. Reluctant, and sort of searching his memory, too. No wonder. Well, there's only one place it can have gone to now: right back where it came from."

"The planet? It can't."

"No. McCoy's cabin." He started to get up, but Spock lifted a hand sharply.

"Better look first, Captain. It may not have killed him yet, and if we alarm it—"

"You're right." Quickly, Kirk dialed in the intercom to McCoy's cabin, and after only a slight hesitation, punched the override button which would give him vision without sounding the buzzer on the other end.

McCoy was there. He was there twice: a sleeping McCoy on the bunk, and another one standing just inside the closed doorway, looking across the room. The standing form moved, passing in front of the hidden camera and momentarily blocking the view. Then it came back into the frame—but no longer as McCoy. It was Nancy.

She sat down on the bed and shook the sleeping doctor. He muttered, but refused to wake.

"Leonard," Nancy's voice said. "It's me. Nancy. Wake up. Please wake up. Help me."

Kirk had to admire the performance. What he was seeing was no doubt an alien creature, but its terror was completely convincing. Quite possibly it *was* in terror; in any event, the human form conveyed it as directly as a blow.

She shook McCoy again. He blinked his eyes groggily, and then sat up.

"Nancy! What's this? How long have I been sleeping?"

"Help me, Leonard."

"What's wrong? You're frightened."

"I am, I am," she said. "Please help me. They want to kill me!"

"Who?" McCoy said. "Easy. Nobody's going to hurt you."

"That's enough," Kirk said, unconsciously lowering

his voice, though the couple on the screen could not hear him. "Luckily, the thing's trying to persuade him of something instead of killing him. Let's get down there fast, before it changes its mind."

Moments later, they burst into McCoy's cabin. The surgeon and the girl swung toward them. "Nancy" cried out.

"Get away from her, Bones," Kirk said, holding his gun rock steady.

"What? What's going on here, Jim?"

"That isn't Nancy, Bones."

"It isn't? Of course it is. Are you off your rocker?"

"It killed two crewmen."

"Bierce, too," Spock put in, his own gun leveled. "*It?*"

"It," Kirk said. "Let me show you."

Kirk held out his free hand, unclenching it slowly. In the palm was a little heap of white crystals, diminishing at the edges from perspiration. "Look, Nancy," he said. "Salt. Free for the taking. Pure, concentrated salt."

Nancy took a hesitant step toward him, then stopped.

"Leonard," she said in a low voice. "Send him away. If you love me, make him go away."

"By all means," McCoy said harshly. "This is crazy behavior, Jim. You're frightening her."

"Not fright," Kirk said. "Hunger. Look at her!"

The creature, as if hypnotized, took another step forward. Then, without the slightest warning, there was a hurricane of motion. Kirk had a brief impression of a blocky body, man-sized but not the least like a man, and of suction-cup tentacles reaching for his face. Then there was a blast of sound and he fell.

It took a while for both Kirk and McCoy to recover— the captain from the nimbus of Spock's close-range phaser bolt, McCoy from emotional shock. By the time they were all back on the bridge, Bierce's planet was receding.

"The salt was an inspiration," Spock said. "Evidently the creature only hunted when it couldn't get the pure stuff; that's how Bierce kept it in control."

"I don't think the salt supply was the only reason why the race died out, though," Kirk said. "It wasn't really very intelligent—didn't use its advantages nearly as well as it might have."

"They could well have been residual," Spock suggested. "We still have teeth and nails, but we don't bite and claw much these days."

"That could well be. There's one thing I don't understand, though. How did it get into your cabin in the first place, Bones? Or don't you want to talk about it?"

"I don't mind," McCoy said. "Though I do feel like six kinds of a fool. It was simple. She came in just after I'd taken the tranquilizer and was feeling a little afloat. She said she didn't love her husband any more—wanted me to take her back to Earth. Well ... it was a real thing I had with Nancy, long ago. I wasn't hard to tempt, especially with the drug already in my system. And later on, while I was asleep, she must have given me another dose—otherwise I couldn't have slept through all the exitement, the general quarters call and so on. It just goes to prove all over again—never mess with civilians."

"A good principle," Kirk agreed. "Unfortunately, an impossible one to live by."

"There's something *I* don't understand, though," McCoy added. "The creature and Bierce had Spock all alone in Bierce's cabin—and from what I've found during the dissection, it was twice as strong as a man anyhow. How did you get out, Mr. Spock, without losing anything but your gun?"

Spock smiled. "Fortunately, my ancestors spawned in quite another ocean than yours, Dr. McCoy," he said. "My blood salts are quite different from yours. Evidently, I wasn't appetizing enough."

"Of course," McCoy said. He looked over at Kirk. "You still look a little pensive, Jim. Is there still something else wrong?"

"Mmm?" Kirk said. "Wrong? No, not exactly. I was just thinking about the buffalo."

Balance of Terror

When the Romulan outbreak began, Capt. James Kirk was in the chapel of the starship *Enterprise,* waiting to perform a wedding.

He could, of course, have declined to do any such thing. Not only was he the only man aboard the starship empowered to perform such a ceremony—and many others even less likely to occur to a civilian—but both the participants were part of the ship's complement: Specialist (phaser) Robert Tomlinson and Spec. 2nd Cl. (phaser) Angela Martine.

Nevertheless, the thought of refusing hadn't occurred to him. Traveling between the stars, even at "relativistic" or near-light speeds, was a long-drawn-out process at best. One couldn't forbid or even ignore normal human relationships over such prolonged hauls, unless one was either a martinet or a fool, and Kirk did not propose to be either.

And in a way, nothing could be more symbolic of his function, and that of the *Enterprise* as a whole, than a marriage. Again because of the vast distances and time lapses involved, the starships were effectively the only fruitful links between the civilized planets. Even interstellar radio, which was necessarily faster, was subject to a dozen different kinds of interruptions, could carry no goods, and in terms of human contact was in every way less satisfactory. On the other hand, the starships were as fructifying as worker bees; they carried supplies, medical help, technical knowledge, news of home, and—above all—the sight and touch of other people.

It was for the same complex of reasons that there was a chapel aboard the *Enterprise*. Designed by some groundlubber in the hope of giving offense to nobody (or, as the official publicity had put it, "to accommodate all faiths of all planets," a task impossible on the face of it), the chapel was simplified and devoid of symbols to the point of insipidity; but its very existence acknowledged that even the tightly designed *Enterprise* was a world in itself, and as such had to recognize that human beings often have religious impulses.

The groom was already there when Kirk entered, as were about half a dozen crew members, speaking *sotto voce*. Nearby, Chief Engineer Scott was adjusting a small television camera; the ceremony was to be carried throughout the intramural network, and outside the ship, too, to the observer satellites in the Romulus-Remus neutral zone. Scotty could more easily have assigned the chore to one of his staff, but doing it himself was his acknowledgment of the solemnity of the occasion—his gift to the bride, as it were. Kirk grinned briefly. Ship's air was a solid mass of symbols today.

"Everything under control, Scotty?"

"Can't speak for the groom, sir, but all's well otherwise."

"Very good."

The smile faded a little, however, as Kirk moved on toward the blankly nondenominational altar. It bothered him a little—not exactly consciously, but somewhere at the back of his conscience—to be conducting an exercise like this so close to the neutral zone. The Romulans had once been the most formidable of enemies. But then, not even a peep had been heard from them since the neutral zone had been closed around their system, fifty-odd years ago. Even were they cooking something venomous under there, why should they pick today to try it—and with a heavily armed starship practically in their back yards?

Scotty, finishing up with the camera, smoothed down his hair self-consciously; he was to give the bride away. There was a murmur of music from the intercom—Kirk could only suppose it was something traditional, since he himself was tune-deaf—and Angela came in, flanked by her bridesmaid, Yeoman Janice Rand. Scott offered her his arm. Tomlinson and his best man were already in position. Kirk cleared his throat experimentally.

And at that moment, the ship's alarm went off.

Angela went white. Since she was new aboard, she might never have heard the jarring blare before, but she obviously knew what it was. Then it was replaced by the voice of Communications Officer Uhura:

"Captain Kirk to the bridge! Captain Kirk to the bridge!"

But the erstwhile pastor was already out the door at a dead run.

Spock, the First Officer, was standing beside Lieutenant Uhura's station as Kirk and his engineer burst onto the bridge. Spock, the product of marriage between an earth woman and a father on Vulcan—not the imaginary Solar world of that name, but a planet of 40 Eridani—did not come equipped with Earth-human emotions, and Lieutenant Uhura had the impassivity of most Bantu women; but the air was charged with tension nonetheless. Kirk said: "What's up?"

"It's Commander Hansen, outpost satellite four zero two three," Spock said precisely. "They've picked up clear pips of an intruder in the neutral zone."

"Identification?"

"None yet, but the engine pattern is modern. Not a Romulan vessel, apparently."

"Excuse me, Mr. Spock," a voice said from the comm board. "I'm overhearing you. We have a sighting now. The vessel is modern—but the markings are Romulan."

Kirk shouldered forward and took the microphone from Lieutenant Uhura's hand. "This is Captain Kirk. Have you challenged it, Hansen?"

"Affirmative. No acknowledgment. Can you give us support, Captain? You are the only starship in this sector."

"Affirmative."

"We're clocking their approach visually at . . ." Hansen's voice died for a moment. Then: "Sorry, just lost them. Disappeared from our monitors."

"Better transmit your monitor picture. Lieutenant Uhura, put it on our bridge viewscreen."

For a moment, the screen showed nothing but a scan of stars, fading into faint nebulosity in the background. Then, suddenly, the strange ship was there. Superficially, it looked much like an *Enterprise*-class starship; a domed disc, seemingly coming at the screen nearly edge-on—though of course it was actually approaching the satellite, not the *Enterprise*. Its size, however, was impossible to guess without a distance estimate.

"Full magnification, Lieutenant Uhura."

The stranger seemed to rush closer. Scott pointed mutely, and Kirk nodded. At this magnification, the stripes along the underside were unmistakable: broad shadows suggesting a bird of prey with half-spread wings. Romulan, all right.

From S-4023, Hansen's voice said urgently: "Got it again! Captain Kirk, can you see—"

"We see it."

But even as he spoke, the screen suddenly turned white, then dimmed as Uhura backed it hastily down the intensity scale. Kirk blinked and leaned forward tensely.

The alien vessel had launched a torpedolike bolt of blinding light from its underbelly. Moving with curious deliberateness, as though it were traveling at the speed of light in some other space but was loafing sinfully in this one, the dazzling bolt swelled in S-4023's camera lens, as if it were bound to engulf the *Enterprise* as well.

"She's opened fire!" Hansen's voice shouted. "Our screen's failed—we're—"

The viewscreen of the *Enterprise* spat doomsday light throughout the control room. The speaker squawked desperately and went dead.

"Battle stations," Kirk told Uhura, very quietly. "General alarm. Mr. Spock, full ahead and intercept."

Nobody had ever seen a live Romulan. It was very certain that "Romulan" was not their name for themselves, for such fragmentary evidence as had been pieced together from wrecks, after they had erupted from the Romulus-Remus system so bloodily a good seventy-five years ago, suggested that they'd not even been native to the planet, let alone a race that could have shared Earthly conventions of nomenclature. A very few bloated bodies recovered from space during that war had proved to be humanoid, but of the hawklike Vulcanite type rather than the Earthly anthropoid. The experts had guessed that the Romulans might once have settled on their adopted planet as a splinter group from some mass migration, thrown off, rejected by their less militaristic fellows as they passed to some more peaceful settling, to some less demanding kind of new world. Neither Romulus nor Remus, twin planets whirling around a common center in a Trojan relationship to a white-dwarf sun, could have proved attractive to any race that did not love hardships for their own sakes.

But almost all this was guesswork, unsupported either by history or by interrogation. The Vulcanite races who were part of the Federation claimed to know nothing of the Romulans; and the Romulans themselves had never allowed any prisoners to be taken—suicide, apparently, was a part of their military tradition—nor had they ever taken any. All that was known for sure was that the Romulans had come boiling out of their crazy little planetary system on no apparent provocation, in primitive, clumsy cylindrical ships that should have been clay pigeons for the Federation's navy and yet in fact took twenty-five years to drive back to their home world—twenty-five years of increasingly merciless slaughter on both sides.

The neutral zone, with its sphere of observer satellites, had been set up around the Romulus-Remus system after that, and for years had been policed with the utmost vigilance. But for fifty years nothing had come out of it—not even a signal, let alone a ship. Perhaps the Romulans were still nursing their wounds and perfecting their grievances and their weapons—or perhaps they had learned their lesson and given up—or perhaps they were just tired, or decadent. . . .

Guesswork. One thing was certain now. Today, they had come out again—or one ship had.

The crew of the *Enterprise* moved to battle stations with a smooth efficiency that would hardly have suggested to an outsider that most of them had never heard a shot fired in anger. Even the thwarted bridal couple was at the forward phaser consoles, as tensely ready now to launch destruction as they had been for creation only a few hours before.

But there was nothing to fire at in the phaser sights yet. On the bridge, Kirk was in the captain's chair, Spock and Scott to either side of him. Sulu was piloting; Second Officer Stiles navigating. Lieutenant Uhura, as usual, was at the comm board.

"No response from satellites four zero two three, two four or two five," she said. "No trace to indicate any are still in orbit. Remaining outposts still in position. No sightings of intruding vessel. Sensor readings normal. Neutral zone, zero."

"Tell them to stay alert and report anything abnormal."

"Yes, sir."

"Entering four zero two three's position area," Sulu said.

"Lieutenant Uhura?"

"Nothing, sir. No, I'm getting a halo effect here now. Debris, I'd guess—metallic, finally divided, and still scattering. The radiant point's obviously where the satellite should be; I'm running a computer check now, but—"

"But there can't be much doubt about it," Kirk said heavily. "They pack a lot more punch than they did fifty years ago—which somehow doesn't surprise me much."

"What *was* that weapon, anyhow?" Stiles whispered.

"We'll check before we guess," Kirk said. "Mr. Spock, put out a tractor and bring me in some of that debris. I want a full analysis—spectra, stress tests, X-ray diffusion, micro-chemistry, the works. We know what the hull of that satellite used to be made of. I want to know what it's like *now*—and then I want some guesses from the lab on how it got that way. Follow me?"

"Of course, sir," the First Officer said. From any other man it would have been a brag, and perhaps a faintly insulting one at that. From Spock it was simply an utterly reliable statement of fact. He was already on the intercom to the lab section.

"Captain," Uhura said. Her voice sounded odd.

"What is it?"

"I'm getting something here. A mass in motion. Nothing more. Nothing on visual, no radar pip. And no radiation. Nothing but a De Broglie transform in the computer. It could be something very small and dense nearby, or something very large and diffuse far away, like a comet. But the traces don't match for either."

"Navigator?" Kirk said.

"There's a cold comet in the vicinity, part of the Romulus-Remus system," Stiles said promptly. "Bearing 973 galactic east, distance one point three light hours, course roughly convergent—"

"I'd picked that up long ago," Uhura said. "This is something else. Its relative speed to us is one-half light, in toward the neutral zone. It's an electromagnetic field of some kind . . . but no kind I ever saw before. I'm certain it's not natural."

"No, it isn't," Spock said, with complete calmness. He might have been announcing the weather, had there been any out here. "It's an invisibility screen."

Stiles snorted, but Kirk knew from long experience that his half-Vulcanite First Officer never made such flat statements without data to back them. Spock was very odd by Earth-human standards, but he had a mind like a rapier. "Explain," Kirk said.

"The course matches for the vessel that attacked the last satellite outpost to disappear," Spock said. "Not the one we're tracking now, but four zero two five. The whole orbit feeds in along Hohmann D toward an intercept with Romulus. The computer shows that already."

"Lieutenant Uhura?"

"Check," she said, a little reluctantly.

"Second: Commander Hansen lost sight of the enemy vessel when it was right in front of him. It didn't reappear until it was just about to launch its attack. Then it vanished again, and we haven't seen it since. Third: Theoretically, the thing is possible, for a vessel of the size of the *Enterprise,* if you put almost all the ship's power into it; hence, you must become visible if you need power for your phasers, or any other energy weapon."

"And fourth, baloney," Stiles said.

"Not quite, Mr. Stiles," Kirk said slowly. "This would also explain why just one Romulan vessel might venture through the neutral zone, right under the nose of the *Enterprise.* The Romulans may think they can take us on now, and they've sent out one probe to find out."

"A very long chain of inferences, sir," Stiles said, with marked politeness.

"I'm aware of that. But it's the best we've got at the moment. Mr. Sulu, match course and speed exactly with Lieutenant Uhura's blip, and stick with it move for move. But under no circumstances cross after it into the neutral zone without my direct order. Miss Uhura, check all frequencies for a carrier wave, an engine pattern, any sort of transmission besides this De Broglie wave-front—in particular, see if you can overhear any chit-chat between ship and home planet. Mr. Spock and Mr. Scott, I'll see you both directly in the briefing room; I want to review what we know about Romulus. Better call Dr. McCoy in on it, too. Any questions?"

There were none. Kirk said, "Mark and move."

The meeting in the briefing room was still going on when Spock was called out to the lab section. Once he was gone, the atmosphere promptly became more informal; neither Scott nor McCoy liked the Vulcanite, and even Kirk, much though he valued his First Officer, was not entirely comfortable in his presence.

"Do you want me to go away too, Jim?" McCoy said gently. "It seems to me you could use some time to think."

"I think better with you here, Bones. You too, Scotty. But this could be the big one. We've got people from half the planets of the Federation patrolling the neutral zone. If we cross it with a starship without due cause, we may have more than just the Romulans to worry about. That's how civil wars start, too."

"Isn't the loss of three satellites due cause?" Scott said.

"I'd say so, but precisely what knocked out those satellites? A Romulan ship, we say; but can we prove it? Well, no, we say; the thing's invisible. Even Stiles laughs at that, and he's on our side. The Romulans were far behind us in technology the last we saw of them— they only got as far as they did in the war out of the advantage of surprise, plus a lot of sheer savagery. Now, suddenly, they've got a ship as good as ours, *plus* an invisibility screen. I can hardly believe it myself.

"And on the other hand, gentlemen . . . On the other hand, while we sit here debating the matter, they may be about to knock us right out of the sky. It's the usual verge-of-war situation: we're damned if we do, and damned if we don't."

The elevator door slid open. Spock was back. "Sir—"

"All right, Mr. Spock. Shoot."

Spock was carrying a thick fascicle of papers bound to a clip board, held close to his body under one arm. His other hand swung free, but its fist was clenched. The bony Vulcanite face had no expression and could show none, but there was something in his very posture that telegraphed tension.

"Here are the analyses of the debris," he said in his inhumanly even voice. "I shan't bother you with the details unless you ask. The essence of the matter is that the Romulan weapon we saw used on S-4023 seems to be a molecular implosion field."

"Meaning what?" McCoy said roughly.

Spock raised his right fist over the plot board, still clenched. The knuckles and tendons worked for a moment. A fine metallic glitter sifted down onto the table.

"It fatigues metals," he said. "Instantly. The metal crystals lose cohesion, and collapse into dust—like this. After that, anything contained in the metal blows up of itself, because it isn't contained any more. I trust that's clear, Dr. McCoy. If not, I'll try to explain it again."

"Damn you, Spock—"

"Shut up, Bones," Kirk said tiredly. "Mr. Spock, sit down. Now then. We're in no position to fight among ourselves. Evidently we're even worse off than we thought we were. If the facts we have are to be trusted, the Romulans have, first, a practicable invisibility screen, and second, a weapon at the very least comparable to ours."

"Many times superior," Spock said stolidly. "At least in some situations."

"*Both* of these gadgets," McCoy said, "are Mr. Spock's inventions, very possibly. At least in both cases, it's his interpretation of the facts that's panicking us."

"There are no other interpretations available at the moment," Kirk said through thinned lips. "Any argument about that? All right. Then let's see what we can make of them for our side. Scotty, what have *we* got that we can counter with, given that the Romulan gadgets are real? We can't hit an invisible object, and we can't duck an invisible gunner. Where does that leave us?"

"Fully armed, fast and maneuverable," the engineer said. "Also, they aren't quite invisible; Lieutenant Uhura can pick up their De Broglie waves as they move. That means that they must be operating at nearly full power right now, just running away and staying invisible. We've got the edge on speed, and I'd guess that they don't know that our sensors are picking them up."

"Which means that we can outrun them and know—approximately—what they're doing. But we can't out-gun them or see them."

"That's how it looks at the moment," Scott said. "It's a fair balance of power, I'd say, Jim. Better than most commanders can count on in a battle situation."

"This isn't a battle situation yet," Kirk said. "Nor even a skirmish. It's the thin edge of an interstellar war. We don't dare to be wrong."

"We can't be righter than we are with the facts at hand, sir," Spock said.

McCoy's lips twitched. "You're so damned sure—"

A beep from the intercom stopped him. Way up in the middle of the air, Lieutenant Uhura's voice said:

"Captain Kirk."

"Go ahead, Lieutenant," Kirk said, his palms sweating.

"I've got a fix on the target vessel. Still can't see it—but I'm getting voices."

Even McCoy pounded up with them to the bridge. Up there, from the master speaker on the comm board, a strange, muted gabble was issuing, fading in and out and often hashed with static, but utterly incomprehensible even at its best. The voices sounded harsh and only barely human; but that could have been nothing more than the illusion of strangeness produced by an unknown language.

The Bantu woman paid no attention to anything but her instruments. Both her large hands were resting delicately on dial knobs, following the voices in and out, back and forth, trying to keep them in aural focus. Beside her left elbow a tape deck ran, recording the gabble for whatever use it might be later for the Analysis team.

"This appears to be coming off their intercom system," she said into the tape-recorder's mike. "A weak signal with high impedance, pulse-modulated. Worth checking what kind of field would leak such a signal, what kind of filtration spectrum it shows—oh, damn—no, there it is again. Scotty, is that you breathing down my neck?"

"Sure is, dear. Need help?"

"Get the computer to work out this waver-pattern for me. My wrists are getting tired. If we can nail it down, I might get a picture."

Scott's fingers flew over the computer console. Very shortly, the volume level of the gabble stabilized, and Lieutenant Uhura leaned back in her seat with a sigh, wriggling her fingers in mid-air. She looked far from relaxed, however.

"Lieutenant," Kirk said. "Do you think you can really get a picture out of that transmission?"

"Don't know why not," the Communications Officer said, leaning forward again. "A leak that size should be big enough to peg rocks through, given a little luck. They've got visible light blocked, but they've left a lot of other windows open. Anyhow, let's try . . ."

But nothing happened for a while. Stiles came in quietly and took over the computer from Scott, walking carefully and pointedly around Spock. Spock did not seem to notice.

"This is a funny business entirely," McCoy said almost to himself. "Those critters were a century behind us, back when we drove them back to their kennels. But that ship's almost as good as ours. It even *looks* like ours. And the weapons . . ."

"Shut up a minute, please, Dr. McCoy," Lieutenant Uhura said. "I'm beginning to get something."

"Sulu," Kirk said. "Any change in their course?"

"None, sir. Still heading home."

"Eureka!" Lieutenant Uhura crowed triumphantly. "There it is!"

The master screen lit. Evidently, Kirk judged, the picture was being picked up by some sort of monitor camera in the Romulan's control room. That in itself was odd; though the *Enterprise* had monitor cameras almost everywhere, there was none on the bridge—who, after all, would be empowered to watch the Captain?

Three Romulans were in view across the viewed chamber, sitting at scanners, lights from their hooded viewers playing upon their faces. They looked human, or nearly so: lean men, with almond-colored faces, dressed in military tunics which bore wolf's-head emblems. The severe, reddish tone of the bulkheads seemed to accentuate their impassivity. Their heads were encased in heavy helmets.

In the foreground, a man who seemed to be the commanding officer worked in a cockpit-like well. Compared to the bridge of the *Enterprise,* this control room looked cramped. Heavy conduits snaked overhead, almost within touch.

All this, however, was noted in an instant and forgotten. Kirk's attention was focused at once on the commander. His uniform was white, and oddly less decorated than those of his officers. Even more importantly, however, he wore no helmet. And in his build, his stance, his coloring, even the cant and shape of his ears, he was a dead ringer for Spock.

Without taking his eyes from the screen, Kirk could sense heads turning toward the half-Vulcanite. There was a long silence, except for the hum of the engines and the background gabble of the Romulan's conversation. Then Stiles said, apparently to himself:

"So now we know. They got our ship design from spies. They can pass for us . . . or for some of us."

Kirk took no overt notice of the remark. Possibly it had been intended only for his ears, or for nobody's; until further notice he was tentatively prepared to think so. He said:

"Lieutenant Uhura, I want linguistics and cryptography to go to work on that language. If we can break it—"

There was another mutter from Stiles, not intelligible but a good deal louder than before. It was no longer possible to ignore him.

"I didn't quite hear that, Mr. Stiles."

"Only talking to myself, sir."

"Do it louder. I want to hear it."

"It wasn't—"

"Repeat it," Kirk said, issuing each syllable like a bullet. Everyone was watching Kirk and Stiles now except Spock, as though the scene on the screen was no longer of any interest at all.

"All right," Stiles said. "I was just thinking that Mr. Spock could probably translate for us a lot faster than the analysts or the computer could. After all, they're his kind of people. You have only to look at them to see that. We can all see it."

"Is that an accusation?"

Stiles drew a deep breath. "No, sir," he said evenly. "It's an observation. I hadn't intended to make it public, and if it's not useful, I'll withdraw it. But I think it's an observation most of us have already made."

"Your apology doesn't satisfy me for an instant. However, since the point's now been aired, we'll explore it. Mr. Spock, do you understand the language those people are speaking? Much as I dislike Mr. Stiles' imputation, there is an ethnic resemblance between the Romulans and yourself. Is it meaningful?"

"I don't doubt that it is," Spock said promptly. "Most of the poeple in this part of space seem to come from the same stock. The observation isn't new. However, Vulcan has had no more contact than Earth has with the Romulans in historical times; and I certainly don't understand the language. There are suggestions of roots in common with my home language—just as English has some Greek roots. That wouldn't help you to understand Greek from a standing start, though it might help you to figure out something about the language, given time. I'm willing to try it—but I don't hold out much hope of its being useful in time to help us out of our present jam."

In the brief silence which followed, Kirk became aware that the muttering from the screen had stopped. Only a second later, the image of the Romulan bridge had dissolved too.

"They've blocked the leak," Uhura reported. "No way to tell whether or not they knew we were tapping it."

"Keep monitoring it and let me know the instant you pick them up again. Make a copy of your tape for Mr. Spock. Dr. McCoy and Mr. Scott, please come with me to my quarters. Everyone else, bear in mind that we're on continuous alert until this thing is over, one way or another."

Kirk stood up, and seemed to turn toward the elevator. Then, after a carefully calculated pause, he swung on Stiles.

"As for you, Mr. Stiles: Your suggestion may indeed be useful. At the moment, however, I think it perilously close to bigotry, which is a sentiment best kept to yourself. Should you have another such notion, be sure I hear it *before* you air it on the bridge. Do I make myself clear?"

White as milk, Stiles said in a thin voice: "You do, sir."

In his office, Kirk put his feet up and looked sourly at the doctor and his engineer. "As if we didn't have enough trouble," he said. "Spock's a funny customer; he gets everybody's back hair up now and then just on ordinary days; and this ... coincidence ... is at best a damn bad piece of timing."

"If it is a coincidence," McCoy said.

"I think it is, Bones. I trust Spock; he's a good officer. His manners are bad by Earth standards, but I don't think much of Stiles' manners either at the moment. Let's drop the question for now. I want to know what to do. The Romulan appears to be running. He'll hit the neutral zone in a few hours. Do we keep on chasing him?"

"You've got a war on your hands if you do," McCoy said. "As you very well know. Maybe a civil war."

"Exactly so. On the other hand, we've already lost three outpost satellites. That's sixty lives—besides all that expensive hardware...I went to school with Hansen, did you know that? Well, never mind. Scotty, what do you think?"

"I don't want to write off sixty lives," Scott said. "But we've got nearly four hundred on board the *Enterprise,* and I don't want to write them off either. We've got no defense against that Romulan weapon, whatever it is—and the phasers can't hit a target they can't see. It just might be better to let them run back inside the neutral zone, file a complaint with the Federation, and wait for a navy to take over. That would give us more time to analyze these gadgets of theirs, too."

"And the language and visual records," McCoy added. "Invaluable, unique stuff—all of which will be lost if we force an engagement and lose it."

"Prudent and logical," Kirk admitted. "I don't agree with a word of it, but it would certainly look good in the log. Anything else?"

"What else do you need?" McCoy demanded. "Either it makes sense or it doesn't. I trust you're not suddenly going all bloody-minded on me, Jim."

"You know better than that. I told you I went to school with Hansen; and I've got kids on board here who were about to get married when the alarm went off. Glory doesn't interest me, either, *or* the public record. *I want to block this war*. That's the charge that's laid upon me now. The only question is, How?"

He looked gloomily at his toes. After a while he added:

"This Romulan irruption is clearly a test of strength. They have two weapons. They came out of the neutral zone and challenged a star ship with them—with enough slaughter and destruction to make sure we couldn't ignore the challenge. It's also a test of our determination. They want to know if we've gone soft since we beat them back the last time. Are we going to allow our friends and property to be destroyed just because the odds seem to be against us? How much peace will the Romulans let us enjoy if we play it safe now—especially if we let them duck back into a neutral zone they've violated themselves? By and large, I don't think there's much future in that, for us, for the Earth, for the Federation—*or even for the Romulans*. The time to pound that lesson home is now."

"You may be right," Scott said. "I never thought I'd say so, but I'm glad it isn't up to me."

"Bones?"

"Let it stand. I've one other suggestion, though. It might improve morale if you'd marry those two youngsters from the phaser deck."

"Do you think this is exactly a good time for that?"

"I'm not sure there's ever a right time. But if you care for your crew—and I know damn well you do—that's precisely the right way to show it at the moment. An instance of love on an eve of battle. I trust I don't embarrass you."

"You do, Doctor," Kirk said, smiling, "but you're right. I'll do it. But it's going to have to be quick."

"Nothing lasts very long," McCoy said enigmatically.

On the bridge, nothing seemed to have happened. It took Kirk a long moment to realize that the conference in his office had hardly taken ten minutes. The Romulan vessel, once more detectable only by the De Broglie waves of its motion, was still apparently fleeing for the neutral zone, but at no great pace.

"It's possible that their sensors can't pick us up either through that screen," Spock said.

"That, or he's trying to draw us into some kind of trap," Kirk said. "Either way, we can't meet him in a head-on battle. We need an edge . . . a diversion. Find me one, Mr. Spock."

"Preferably nonfatal," Stiles added. Sulu half turned to him from the pilot board.

"You're so wrong about this," Sulu said, "you've used up all your mistakes for the rest of your life."

"One of us has," Stiles said stiffly.

"Belay that," Kirk said. "Steady as she goes, Mr. Sulu. The next matter on the agenda is the wedding."

"In accordance with space law," Kirk said, "we are gathered together for the purpose of joining this woman, Angela Martine, and this man, Robert Tomlinson, in the bond of matrimony ..."

This time there were no interruptions. Kirk closed his book and looked up.

"... And so, by the powers vested in me as Captain of the U.S.S. *Enterprise*, I now pronounce you man and wife."

He nodded to Tomlinson, who only then remembered to kiss the bride. There was the usual hubbub, not seemingly much muted by the fewness of the spectators. Yeoman Rand rushed up to kiss Angela's cheek; McCoy pumped Tomlinson's hand, slapped him on the shoulder, and prepared to collect his kiss from the bride, but Kirk interposed.

"Captain's privilege, Bones."

But he never made it; the wall speaker checked him. The voice was Spock's.

"Captain—I think I have the diversion you wanted."

"Some days," Kirk said ruefully, "nothing on this ship ever seems to get finished. I'll be right there, Mr. Spock."

Spock's diversion turned out to be the cold comet they had detected earlier—now "cold" no longer, for as it came closer to the central Romulan-Reman sun it had begun to display its plumage. Spock had found it listed in the ephemeris, and a check of its elements with the computer had shown that it would cross between the *Enterprise* and the Romulan 440 seconds from now—not directly between, but close enough to be of possible use.

"We'll use it," Kirk declared promptly. "Mr. Sulu, we'll close at full acceleration at the moment of interposition. Scotty, tell the phaser room we'll want a bracketing salvo; we'll be zeroing on sensors only, and with that chunk of ice nearly in the way, there'll be some dispersion."

"Still, at that range we ought to get at least one hit," Scott said.

"One minute to closing," Spock said.

"Suppose the shot doesn't get through their screen?" Stiles said.

"A distinct possibility," Kirk agreed. "About which we can do exactly nothing."

"Thirty seconds . . . twenty . . . fifteen . . . ten, nine, eight, seven, six, five, four, three, two, one, zero."

The lights dimmed as the ship surged forward and at the same moment, the phaser coils demanded full drain. The comet swelled on the screen.

"All right, Mr. Tomlinson . . . Hit 'em!"

The *Enterprise* roared like a charging lion. An instant later, the lights flashed back to full brightness, and the noise stopped. The phasers had cut out.

"Overload," Spock said emotionlessly. "Main coil burnout." He was already at work, swinging out a panel to check the circuitry. After only a split second of hesitation, Stiles crossed to help him.

"Captain!" Sulu said. "Their ship—it's fading into sight. I think we got a hit—yes, we did!"

"Not good enough," Kirk said grimly, instantly suspecting the real meaning of the Romulan action. "Full retro power! Evasive action!"

But the enemy was still faster. On the screen, a radiant torpedo like the one they had seen destroy Satellite 4023 was scorching toward the *Enterprise*—and this time it was no illusion that the starship was the target.

"No good," Sulu said. "Two minutes to impact."

"Yeoman Rand, jettison recorder buoy in ninety seconds."

"Hold it," Sulu said. "That shot's changing shape—"

Sure enough: the looming bolt seemed to be wavering, flattening. Parts of it were peeling off in tongues of blue energy; its brilliance was dimming. Did it have a range limit—

The bolt vanished from the screen. The *Enterprise* lurched sharply. Several people fell, including Spock—luckily away from the opened instrument panel, which crackled and spat.

"Scotty! Damage report!"

"One hold compartment breached. Minor damage otherwise. Main phaser battery still out of action, until that coil's replaced."

"I think the enemy got it worse, sir," Lieutenant Uhura said. "I'm picking up debris-scattering ahead. Conduits—castings—plastoform shadows—and an echo like the body of a casualty."

There was a ragged cheer, which Kirk silenced with a quick, savage gesture. "Maintain deceleration. Evidently they have to keep their screen down to launch their weapon—and the screen's still down."

"No, they're fading again, Captain," Sulu said. "Last Doppler reading shows they're decelerating too ... Now they're gone again."

"Any pickup from their intercom, Lieutenant Uhura?"

"Nothing, sir. Even the De Broglies are fading. I think the comet's working against us now."

Now what in space did that mean? Fighting with an unknown enemy was bad enough, but when the enemy could become invisible at will— And if that ship got back to the home planet with all its data, there might well be nothing further heard from the Romulans until they came swarming out of the neutral zone by the millions, ready for the kill. That ship had to be stopped.

"Their tactics make sense over the short haul," Kirk said thoughtfully. "They feinted us in with an attack on three relatively helpless pieces, retreated across the center of the board to draw out our power, then made a flank attack and went to cover. Clearly the Romulans play some form of chess. If I had their next move, I'd go across the board again. If they did that, they'd be sitting in our ionization wake right now, right behind us—with reinforcements waiting ahead."

"What about the wreckage, sir?" Uhura said.

"Shoved out the evacuation tubes as a blind—an old trick, going all the way back to submarine warfare. The next time they do that, they may push out a nuclear warhead for us to play with. Lieutenant Sulu, I want a turnover maneuver, to bring the main phaser battery aligned directly astern. Mr. Spock, we can't wait for main coil replacement any longer; go to the phaser deck and direct fire manually. Mr. Stiles, go with him and give him a hand. Fire at my command directly the turnover's been completed. All understood?"

Both men nodded and went out, Stiles a little reluctantly. Kirk watched them go for a brief instant—despite himself, Stiles' suspicion of Spock had infected him, just a little—and then forgot them. The turnover had begun. On the screen, space astern, in the *Enterprise's* ionization wake, seemed as blank as space ahead, in the disturbed gasses of the now-dwindling comet's tail.

Then, for the third time, the Romulan ship began to materialize, precisely where Kirk had suspected it would be—and there was precisely nothing they could do about it yet. The bridge was dead silent. Teeth clenched, Kirk watched the cross-hairs on the screen creep with infinite slowness toward the solidifying wraith of the enemy—

"All right, Spock, *fire!*"

Nothing happened. The suspicion that flared now would not be suppressed. With a savage gesture, Kirk cut in the intercom screen to the phaser deck.

For a moment he could make nothing of what he saw. The screen seemed to be billowing with green vapor. Through it, dimly, Kirk could see two figures sprawled on the floor, near where the phaser boards should have been. Then Stiles came into the field of view, one hand clasped over his nose and mouth. He was trying to reach the boards, but he must have already taken in a lungful of the green gas. Halfway there, he clutched at his throat and fell.

"Scotty! What is that stuff—"

"Coolant fluid," Scott's voice said harshly. "Seal must have cracked—look, there's Spock—"

Spock was indeed on the screen now, crawling on his hands and knees toward the boards. Kirk realized belatedly that the figures on the deck had to be Tomlinson and one of his crew, both dead since the seal had been cracked, probably when the Romulan had hit the *Enterprise* before. On the main screen, another of the Romulan energy bolts was bearing down upon them, with the inexorability of a Fury. Everything seemed to be moving with preternatural slowness.

Then Spock somehow reached the controls, dragged himself to his knees, moved nearly paralyzed fingers over the instruments. He hit the firing button twice, with the edge of his hand, and then fell.

The lights dimmed. The Romulan blew up.

On board the *Enterprise,* there were three dead: Tomlinson, his aide, and Stiles. Angela had escaped; she hadn't been on the deck when the coolant had come boiling out. Escaped—a wife of half a day, a widow for all the rest of her days. Stolidly, Kirk entered it all in the log.

The Second Romulan War was over. And never mind the dead; officially, it had never even begun.

The Naked Time

☆☆☆

Nobody, it was clear, was going to miss the planet when it did break up. Nobody had even bothered to name it; on the charts it was just ULAPG42821DB, a coding promptly shorted by some of the *Enterprise's* junior officers to "La Pig."

It was not an especially appropriate nickname. The planet, a rockball about 10,000 m¹les in diameter, was a frozen, windless wilderness, without so much as a gnarled root or fragment of lichen to relieve the monotony from horizon to purple horizon. But in one way the name fitted: the empty world was too big for its class.

After a relatively short lifetime of a few hundred million years, stresses between its frozen surface and its shrinking core were about to shatter it.

There was an observation station on La Pig, manned by six people. These would have to be got off, and the *Enterprise,* being in the vicinity, got the job. After that, the orders ran, the starship was to hang around and observe the breakup. The data collected would be of great interest to the sliderule boys back on Earth. Maybe some day they would turn the figures into a way to break up a planet at will, people and all.

Captain Kirk, like most line officers, did not have a high opinion of the chairborne arms of his service.

It turned out, however, that there was nobody at all to pick up off La Pig. The observation station was wide open, and the ice had moved inside. Massive coatings of it lay over everything—floors, consoles, even chairs. The doors were frozen open, and all the power was off.

The six members of the station complement were dead. One, in heavy gear, lay bent half over one of the consoles. On the floor at the entrance to one of the corridors was the body of a woman, very lightly clad and more than half iced over. Inspection, however, showed that she had been dead before the cold had got to her; she had been strangled.

In the lower part of the station were the other four. The engineer sat at his post with all the life-support system switches set at OFF, frozen there as though he hadn't given a damn. There was still plenty of power available; he just hadn't wanted it on any more. Two of the others were dead in their beds, which was absolutely normal and expectable considering the temperature. But the sixth and last man had died while taking a shower—fully clothed.

"There wasn't anything else to be seen," Mr. Spock, the officer in charge of the transporter party, later told Captain Kirk. "Except that there were little puddles of water here and there that hadn't frozen, though at that temperature they certainly should have, no matter what they might have held in solution. We brought back a small sample for the lab. The bodies are in our morgue now, still frozen. As for the people, I think maybe this is a job for a playwright, not an official investigation."

"Imagination's a useful talent in a police officer," Kirk commented. "At a venture, I'd guess that something volatile and highly toxic got loose in the station. One of the men got splattered and rushed to the shower hoping to sluice if off, clothes and all. Somebody else opened all the exit ports in an attempt to let the stuff blow out into the outside atmosphere."

"And the strangled woman?"

"Somebody blamed her for the initial accident—which

was maybe just the last of a long chain of carelessnesses, and maybe irritating behavior too, on her part. You know how tempers can get frayed in small isolated crews like this."

"Very good, Captain," Spock said. "Now what about the engineer shutting off the life systems?"

Kirk threw up his hands. "I give up. Maybe he saw that nothing was going to work and decided on suicide. Or more likely I'm completely wrong all down the line. We'd better settle in our observation orbit. Whatever happened down there, apparently the books are closed."

For the record, it was just as well that he said "apparently."

Joe Tormolen, the crewman who had accompanied Mr. Spock to the observation station, was the first to show the signs. He had been eating all by himself in the recreation room—not unusual in itself, for though efficient and reliable, Joe was not very sociable. Nearby, Sulu, the chief pilot, and Navigator Kevin Riley were having an argument over the merits of fencing as exercise, with Sulu of course holding the affirmative. At some point in the discussion, Sulu appealed to Joe for support.

For answer, Joe flew into a white fury, babbling disconnectedly but under high pressure about the six people who had died on La Pig, and the unworthiness of human beings in general to be in space at all. At the height of this frenzied oration, Joe attempted to turn a steak knife on himself.

The resulting struggle was protracted, and because Sulu and Riley naturally misread Joe's intentions—they thought he was going to attack one of them with the knife—Joe succeeded in wounding himself badly. All three were bloodsmeared by the time he was subdued and hauled off to sick bay; at first arrival, the security guards couldn't guess which of the three scuffling figures was the hurt one.

There was no time to discuss the case in any detail; La Pig was already beginning to break up, and Sulu and Riley were needed on the bridge as soon as they could wash up. As the breakup proceeded, the planet's effective mass would change, and perhaps even its center of gravity—accompanied by steady, growing distortion of its extensive magnetic field—so that what had been a stable parking orbit for the *Enterprise* at one moment would become unstable and fragment-strewn the next. The changes were nothing the computer could predict except in rather general orders of magnitude; human brains had to watch and compensate, constantly.

Dr. McCoy's report that Joe Tormolen had died consequently did not reach Kirk for twenty-four hours, and it was another four before he could answer McCoy's request for a consultation. By then, however, the breakup process seemed to have reached some sort of inflection point, where it would simply pause for an hour or so; he could leave the vigil to Sulu and Riley for a short visit to McCoy's office.

"I wouldn't have called you if Joe hadn't been one of the two men down on La Pig," McCoy said directly. "But the case is odd and I don't want to overlook the possibility that there's some connection."

"What's odd about it?"

"Well," McCoy said, "the suicide attempt itself was odd. Joe's self-doubt quotient always rated high, and he was rather a brooding, introspective type; but I'm puzzled about what could have brought it to the surface this suddenly and with this much force.

"And Jim, he shouldn't have died. He had intestinal damage, but I closed it all up neatly and cleaned out the peritoneum; there was no secondary infection. He died anyhow, and I don't know of what."

"Maybe he just gave up," Kirk suggested.

"I've seen that happen. But I can't put it on a death certificate. I have to have a proximate cause, like toxemia or a clot in the brain. Joe just seemed to have a generalized circulatory failure, from no proximate cause at all. And those six dead people on La Pig are not reassuring."

"True enough. What about that sample Spock brought back?"

McCoy shrugged. "Anything's possible, I suppose—but as far as we can tell, that stuff's just water, with some trace minerals that lower its freezing point a good deal. We're handling it with every possible precaution, it's bacteriologically clean—which means no viruses, either—and very nearly chemically pure. I've about concluded that it's a blind alley, though of course I'm still trying to think of new checks to run on it; we all are."

"Well, I'll keep an eye on Spock," Kirk said. "He was the only other man who was down there—though his metabolism's so different that I don't know what I'll be looking for. And in the meantime, we'll just have to hope it was a coincidence."

He went out. As he turned from the door, he was startled to see Sulu coming down a side corridor, not yet aware of Kirk. Evidently he had just come from the gym, for his velour shirt was off, revealing a black tee-shirt, and he had a towel around his neck. He was carrying a fencing foil with a tip protector on it under his arm, and he looked quite pleased with himself—certainly nothing like a man who was away from his post in an alert.

He swung the foil so that it pointed to the ceiling, then let it slip down between his hands so that the capped end was directly before his face. After a moment's study, he took the cap off. Then he took the weapon by the hilt and tested its heft.

. "Sulu!"

The pilot jumped back and hit lightly in the guard position. The point of the foil described small circles in the air between the two men.

"Aha!" Sulu said, almost gleefully. "Queen's guard or Richelieu's man? Declare yourself!"

"Sulu, what's this? You're supposed to be on station."

Sulu advanced one pace with the crab-step of the fencer.

"You think to outwit me, eh? Unsheathe your weapon!"

"That's enough," Kirk said sharply. "Report yourself to sick bay."

"And leave you the bois? Nay, rather—"

He made a sudden lunge. Kirk jumped back and snatched out his phaser, setting it to "stun" with his thumb in the same motion, but Sulu was too quick for him. He leapt for a recess in the wall where there was an access ladder to the 'tween-hulls catwalks, and vanished up it. From the vacated manhole his voice echoed back:

"Cowarrrrrrrrrrrrd!"

Kirk made the bridge on the double. As he entered, Uhura was giving up the navigator's position to another crewman and moving back to her communications console. There was already another substitute in Sulu's chair. Kirk said, "Where's Riley?"

"Apparently he just wandered off," Spock said, surrendering the command chair to Kirk in his turn. "Nobody but Yeoman Harris here saw him go."

"Symptoms?" Kirk asked the helmsman.

"He wasn't violent or anything, sir. I asked where Mr. Sulu was and he began to sing, 'Have no fear, Riley's here.' Then he said he was sorry for me that I wasn't an Irishman—in fact I am, sir—and said he was going for a turn on the battlements."

"Sulu's got it too," Kirk said briefly. "Chased me with a sword on level two, corridor three, then bolted between the hulls. Lieutenant Uhura, tell Security to locate and confine them both. I want every crewman who comes in contact with them medically checked."

"Psychiatrically, I would suggest, Captain," Spock said.

"Explain."

"This siezure, whatever it is, seems to force buried self-images to the surface. Tormolen was a depressive; it drove him down to the bottom of his cycle and below it, so he suicided. Riley fancies himself a descendant of his Irish kings. Sulu at heart is an eighteenth-century swashbuckler."

"All right. What's the present condition of the planet?"

"Breaking faster than predicted," Spock said. "As of now we've got a 2 per cent fall increment."

"Stabilize." He turned to his own command board, but the helmsman's voice jerked his attention back.

"Sir, the helm doesn't answer."

"Fire all ventral verniers then. We'll rectify orbit later."

The helmsman hit the switch. Nothing happened.

"Verniers also dead, sir."

"Main engines: warp one!" Kirk rasped.

"That'll throw us right out of the system," Spock observed, as if only stating a mild inconvenience.

"Can't help that."

"No response, sir," the helmsman said.

"Engine room, acknowledge!" Spock said into the intercom. "Give us power. Our controls are dead."

Kirk jerked a thumb at the elevator. "Mr. Spock, find out what's going on down there."

Spock started to move, but at the same time the elevator door slid aside, and Sulu was advancing, foil in hand. "Richelieu!" he said. "At last!"

"Sulu," Kirk said, "put down that damned—"

"For honor, Queen and France!" Sulu lunged directly at Spock, who in sheer unbelief almost let himself be run through. Kirk tried to move in but the needlepoint flicked promptly in his direction. "Now, foul Richelieu—"

He was about to lunge when he saw Uhura trying to circle behind him. He spun; she halted.

"Aha, fair maiden!"

"Sorry, neither," Uhura said. She threw a glance deliberately over Sulu's left shoulder; as he jerked in that direction, Spock's hand caught him on the right shoulder with the Vulcanian nerve pinch. Sulu went down on the deck like a sack of flour.

Forgetting his existence instantly, Kirk whirled on the intercom. "Mr. Scott! We need power! Scott! Engine room, acknowledge!"

In a musical tenor, the intercom said indolently: "You rang?"

"Riley?" Kirk said, trying to repress his fury.

"This is Capt. Kevin Thomas Riley of the Starship *Enterprise*. And who would I have the honor of speakin' to?"

"This is Kirk, dammit."

"Kirk who? Sure and I've got no such officer."

"Riley, this is Captain Kirk. Get out of the engine room, Navigator. Where's Scott?"

"Now hear this, cooks," Riley said. "This is your captain and I'll be wantin' double portions of ice cream for the crew. Captain's compliments, in honor of St. Kevin's Day. And now, your Captain will render an appropriate selection."

Kirk bolted for the elevator. Spock moved automatically to the command chair. "Sir," he said, "at our present rate of descent we have less than twenty minutes before we enter the planet's exosphere."

"All right," Kirk said grimly. "I'll see what I can do about that monkey. Stand by to apply power the instant you get it."

The elevator doors closed on him. Throughout the ship, Riley's voice began to bawl: "I'll take you home again, Kathleen." He was no singer.

It would have been funny, had it not been for the fact that the serenade had the intercom system completely tied up; that the seizure, judging by Joe Tormolen, was followed by a reasonless death; and that the *Enterprise* itself was due shortly to become just another battered lump in a whirling, planet-sized mass of cosmic rubble.

Scott and two crewmen were outside the engine room door, running a sensor around its edge, as Kirk arrived. Scott looked quickly at the Captain, and then back at the job.

"Trying to get this open, sir," he said. "Riley ran in, said you wanted us on the bridge, then locked us out. We heard you talking to him on the intercom."

"He's cut off both helm and power," Kirk said. "Can you by-pass him and work from the auxiliary?"

"No, Captain, he's hooked everything through the main panel in there." Scott prodded one of the crewmen. "Get up to my office and pull the plans for this bulkhead here. If we've got to cut, I don't want to go through any circuitry." The crewman nodded and ran.

"Can you give us battery power on the helm, at least?" Kirk said. "It won't check our fall but at least it'll keep us stabilized. We've got maybe nineteen minutes, Scotty."

"I heard. I can try it."

"Good." Kirk started back for the bridge.

"And tears be-dim your loving eyes . . ."

On the bridge, Kirk snapped, "Can't you cut off that noise?"

"No, sir," Lieutenant Uhura said. "He can override any channel from the main power panels there."

"There's one he can't override," Kirk said. "Mr. Spock, seal off all ship sections. If this is a contagion, maybe we can stop it from spreading, and at the same time—"

"I follow you," Spock said. He activated the servos for the sector bulkheads. Automatically, the main alarm went off, drowning Riley out completely. When it quit, there was a brief silence. Then Riley's voice said:

"Lieutenant Uhura, this is Captain Riley. You interrupted my song. That was petty of you. No ice cream for you."

"Seventeen minutes left, sir," Spock said.

"Attention crew," Riley's voice went on. "There will be a formal dance in the ship's bowling alley at 1900 hours. All personnel will have a ball." There was a skirl of gleeful laughter. "For the occasion all female crewmen will be issued one pint of perfume from ship's stores. All male crewmen will be raised one pay grade to compensate. Stand by for further goodies."

"Any report on Sulu before the intercom got blanketed?" Kirk said.

"Dr. McCoy had him in sick bay under heavy tranquilization," Lieutenant Uhura said. "He wasn't any worse then, but all tests were negative . . . I got the impression that the surgeon had some sort of idea, but he was cut off before he could explain it."

"Well, Riley's the immediate problem now."

A runner came in and saluted. "Sir, Mr. Scott's compliments and you have a jump circuit from batteries to helm control now. Mr Scott has resumed cutting into the engine room. He says he should have access in fourteen minutes, sir."

"Which is just the margin we have left," Kirk said. "And it'll take three minutes to tune the engines to full power again. Captain's compliments to Mr. Scott and tell him to cut in any old way and not worry about cutting any circuits but major leads."

"Now hear this," Riley's voice said. "In future all female crew members will let their hair hang loosely down over their shoulders and will use restraint in putting on make-up. Repeat, women should not look made up."

"Sir," Spock said in a strained voice.

"One second. I want two security guards to join Mr. Scott's party. Riley may be armed."

"I've already done that," Spock said. "Sir—"

"...Across the ocean wide and deep..."

"Sir, I feel ill," Spock said formally. "Request permission to report to sick bay."

Kirk clapped a hand to his forehead. "Symptoms?"

"Just a general malaise, sir. But in view of—"

"Yes, yes. But you can't *get* to sick bay; the sections are all sealed off."

"Request I be locked in my quarters, then, sir. I can reach those."

"Permission granted. Somebody find him a guard." As Spock went out, another dismaying thought struck Kirk. Suppose McCoy had the affliction now, whatever it was? Except for Spock and the now-dead Tormolen, he had been exposed to it longest, and Spock could be supposed to be unusually resistant. "Lieutenant Uhura, you might as well abandon that console, it's doing us no good at the moment. Find yourself a length of telephone cable and an eavesdropper, and go between hulls to the hull above the sick bay. You'll be able to hear McCoy but not talk back; get his attention, and answer him, by prisoners' raps. Relay the conversation to me by pocket transmitter. Mark and move"

"Yes, *sir*."

Her exit left the bridge empty except for Kirk. There was nothing he could do but pace and watch the big screen. Twelve minutes.

Then a buzzer went off in Kirk's back pocket. He yanked out his communicator.

"Kirk here."

"Lieutenant Uhura, sir. I've established contact with Doctor McCoy. He says he believes he has a partial solution, sir."

"Ask him what he means by partial."

There was an agonizing wait while Uhura presumably spelled out this message by banging on the inner hull. The metal was thick; probably she was using a hammer, and even so the raps would come through only faintly.

"Sir, he wants to discharge something—some sort of gas, sir—into the ship's ventilating system. He says he can do it from sick bay and that it will spread rapidly. He says it worked on Lieutenant Sulu and presumably will cure anybody else who's sick—but he won't vouch for its effect on healthy crew members."

"That sounded like typical McCoy caution, but— ask him how he feels himself."

Another long wait. Then: "He says he felt very ill, sir, but is all right now, thanks to the antidote."

That might be true and it might not. If McCoy himself had the illness, there would be no predicting what he might actually be preparing to dump into the ship's air. On the other hand, to refuse him permission wouldn't necessarily stop him, either. If only that damned singing would stop! It made thinking almost impossible.

"Ask him to have Sulu say something; see if he sounds sane to you."

Another wait. Only ten minutes left now—three of which would have to be used for tune-up. And no telling how fast McCoy's antidote would spread, or how long it would need to take hold, either.

"Sir, he says Lieutenant Sulu is exhausted and he won't wake him, under the discretion granted him by his commission."

McCoy had that discretion, to be sure. But it could also be the cunning blind of a deranged mind.

"All right," Kirk said heavily. "Tell him to go ahead with it."

"Aye aye, sir."

Uhura's carrier wave clicked out and Kirk pocketed his transceiver, feeling utterly helpless. Nine minutes.

Then, Riley's voice faltered. He appeared to have forgotten some of the words of his interminable song. Then he dropped a whole line. He tried to go on, singing "La, la, la," instead, but in a moment that died away too.

Silence.

Kirk felt his own pulse, and sounded himself subjectively. Insofar as he could tell, there was nothing the matter with him but a headache which he now realized he had had for more than an hour. He strode quickly to Uhura's console and rang the engine room.

There was a click from the g.c. speakers, and Riley's voice said hesitantly: "Riley here."

"Mr. Riley, this is Kirk. Where are you?"

"Sir, I . . . I seem to be in the engine room. I'm . . . off post, sir."

Kirk drew a deep breath. "Never mind that. Give us power right away. Then open the door and let the chief engineer in. Stand out of the way when you do it, because he's trying to cut in with a phaser at full power. Have you got all that?"

"Yes, sir. Power, then the door—and stand back. Sir, what's this all about?"

"Never mind now, just do it."

"Yes, sir."

Kirk opened the bulkhead override. At once, there was the heavy rolling sound of the emergency doors between the sections opening, like a stone being rolled back from a tomb. Hitting the general alarm button, Kirk bawled: "All officers to the bridge! Crash emergency, six minutes! Mark and move!"

At the same time, the needles on the power board began to stir. Riley had activated the engines. A moment later, his voice, filled with innocent regret, said into the general air:

"Now there won't be a dance in the bowling alley to-night."

Once a new orbit around the disintegrating mass of La Pig had been established, Kirk found time to question McCoy. The medico looked worn down to a nubbin, and small wonder; his had been the longest vigil of all. But he responded with charactertistic indirection.

"Know anything about cactuses, Jim?"

"Only what everybody knows. They live in the desert and they stick you. Oh yes, and some of them store water."

"Right, and that last item's the main one. Also, cactuses that have been in museum cases for fifty or even seventy years sometimes astonish the museum curators by sprouting. Egyptian wheat that's been in tombs for thousands of years will sometimes germinate, too."

Kirk waited patiently. McCoy would get to the point in his own good time.

"Both those things happen because of a peculiar form of storage called *bound water*. Ordinary mineral crystals like copper sulfate often have water hitched to their molecules, loosely; that's water-of-crystallization. With it, copper sulfate is a pretty blue gem, though poisonous; without it, it's a poisonous green powder. Well, organic molecules can bind water much more closely, make it really a part of the molecule instead of just loosely hitched to it. Over the course of many years, that water will come out of combination and become available to the cactus or the grain of wheat as a liquid, and then life begins all over again."

"An ingenious arrangement," Kirk said. "But I don't see how it nearly killed us all."

"It was in that sample of liquid Mr. Spock brought back, of course—a catalyst that *promoted* water-binding. If it had nothing else to bind to, it would bind even to itself. Once in the bloodstream, the catalyst began complexing the blood-serum. First it made the blood more difficult to extract nutrients from, beginning with blood sugar, which starved the brain—hence the psychiatric symptoms. As the process continued, it made the blood too thick to pump, especially through the smaller capillaries—hence Joe's death by circulatory collapse.

"Once I realized what was happening, I had to figure out a way to poison the catalysis. The stuff was highly contagious, through the perspiration, or blood, or any other body fluid; and catalysts don't take part in any chemical reaction they promote, so the original amount was always present to be passed on. I think this one may even have multiplied, in some semi-viruslike fashion. Anyhow, the job was to alter the chemical nature of the catalyst—poison it—so it wouldn't promote that reaction any more. I almost didn't find the proper poison in time, and as I told Lieutenant Uhura through the wall, I wasn't sure what effect the poison itself would have on healthy people. Luckily, none."

"Great Galaxy," Kirk said. "That reminds me of something. Spock invalided himself off duty just before the tail end of the crisis and he's not back. Lieutenant Uhura, call Mr. Spock's quarters."

"Yes, sir."

The switch clicked. Out of the intercom came a peculiarly Arabic howl—the noise of the Vulcanian musical instrument Spock liked to practice in his cabin, since nobody else on board could stand to listen to it. Along with the noise, Spock's rough voice was crooning:

"Alab, wes-craunish, sprai pu ristu,
Or en r'ljiik majiir auooo—"

Kirk winced. "I can't tell whether he's all right or not," he said. "Nobody but another Vulcanian could. But since he's not on duty during a crash alert, maybe your antidote did something to him it didn't do to us. Better go check him."

"Soon as I find my earplugs."

McCoy left. From Spock's cabin, the voice went on:

"Rijii, bebe, p'salku pirtu,

Fror om—"

The voice rose toward an impassioned climax and Kirk cut the circuit. Rather than that, he would almost rather have "I'll take you home again, Kathleen," back again.

On the other hand, if Riley had sounded like that to Spock, maybe Spock had needed no other reason for feeling unwell. With a sigh, Kirk settled back to watch the last throes of La Pig. The planet was now little better than an irregularly bulging cloud of dust, looking on the screen remarkably like a swelling and disintegrating human brain.

The resemblance, Kirk thought, was strictly superficial. Once a planet started disintegrating, it was through. But brains weren't like that.

Given half a chance, they pulled themselves together. Sometimes.

Miri

✩✩

Any SOS commands instant attention in space, but
there was very good reason why this one created special
interest on the bridge of the *Enterprise*. To begin with,
there was no difficulty in pinpointing its source, for it
came not from any ship in distress, but from a planet,
driven out among the stars at the 21-centimeter frequency by generators far more powerful than even the
largest starship could mount.

A whole planet in distress? But there were bigger
surprises to come. The world in question was a member of
the solar system of 70 Ophiucus, a sun less than fifteen
light-years away from Earth, so that in theory the distress
signals could have been picked up on Earth not much
more than a decade after their launching except for one
handicap: From Earth, 70 Ophiucus is seen against the
backdrop of the Milky Way, whose massed clouds of
excited hydrogen atoms emit 21-centimeter radiation at
some forty times the volume of that coming from the rest
of the sky. Not even the planet's huge, hard-driven generators could hope to punch through that much stellar static
with an intelligible signal, not even so simple a one as an
SOS. Lieutenant Uhura, the communications officer of
the *Enterprise*, picked up the signal only because the
starship was at the time approaching the "local group"—an

arbitrary sphere 100 light-years in diameter with Earth at its center—nearly at right angles to the plane of the galaxy.

All this, however, paled beside the facts about the region dug up by the ship's library computer. For the fourth planet of 70 Ophiucus, the computer said, had been the first extrasolar planet ever colonized by man—by a small but well-equipped group of refugees from the political disaster called the Cold Peace, more than five hundred years ago. It had been visited only once since then. The settlers, their past wrongs unforgotten, had fired on the visitors, and the hint had been taken; after all, the galaxy was full of places more interesting than a backwater like the 70 Ophiucus system, which the first gigantic comber of full-scale exploration had long since passed. The refugees were left alone to enjoy their sullen isolation.

But now they were calling for help.

On close approach it was easy to see why the colonists, despite having been in flight, had settled for a world which might have been thought dangerously close to home. The planet was remarkably Earth-like, with enormous seas covering much of it, stippled and striped with clouds. One hemisphere held a large, roughly lozenge-shaped continent, green and mountainous; the other, two smaller triangular ones, linked by a long archipelago including several islands bigger than Borneo. Under higher magnification, the ship's screen showed the gridworks of numerous cities, and, surprisingly more faintly, the checkerboarding of cultivation.

But no lights showed on the night side, nor did the radio pick up any broadcasts nor any of the hum of a high-energy civilization going full blast. Attempts to communicate, once the *Enterprise* was in orbit, brought no response—only that constantly repeated SOS, which now was beginning to sound suspiciously mechanical.

"Whatever the trouble was," Mr. Spock deduced, "we are evidently too late."

"It looks like it," Captain Kirk agreed. "But we'll go

down and see. Mr. Spock, Dr. McCoy, Yeoman Rand, and two security guards, pick up your gear and report to me in the transporter room."

The landing party materialized by choice in the central plaza of the largest city the screen had shown—but there was no one there. Not entirely surprised, Kirk looked around.

The architecture was roughly like that of the early 2100s, when the colonists had first fled, and apparently had stood unoccupied for almost that long a period. Evidences of the erosion of time were everywhere, in the broken pavements, the towering weeds, the gaping windows, the windrows of dirt and dust. Here and there on the plaza were squat sculptures of flaking rust which had perhaps been vehicles.

"No signs of war," Spock said.

"Pestilence?" McCoy suggested. As if by agreement, both were whispering.

By the dust-choked fountain near which Kirk stood, another antique object lay on its side: a child's tricycle. It too was rusty, but still functional, as though it had been indoors during much of the passage of time which had worn away the larger vehicles. There was a bell attached to the handlebar, and moved by some obscure impulse, Kirk pressed his thumb down on its lever.

It rang with a kind of dull sputter in the still air. The plaintive sound was answered instantly, from behind them, by an almost inhuman scream of rage and anguish.

"Mine! *Mine!*"

They whirled to face the terrible clamor. A humanoid creature was plunging toward them from the shell of the nearest building, flailing its arms and screaming murderously. It was moving too fast for Kirk to make out details. He had only an impression of dirt, tatters, and considerable age, and then the thing had leapt upon McCoy and knocked him down.

Everyone waded in to help, but the creature had the incredible strength of the utterly mad. For a moment

Kirk was face to face with it—an ancient face, teeth gone in a reeking mouth, contorted with wildness and hate, tears brimming from the eyes. Kirk struck, almost at random.

The blow hardly seemed to connect at all, but the creature sobbed and fell to the pocked pavement. He was indeed an old man, clad only in sneakers, shorts, and a ripped and filthy shirt. His skin was covered with multi-colored blotches. There was something else odd about it, too—but what? Was it as wrinkled as it should be?

Still sobbing, the old head turned and looked toward the tricycle, and an old man's shaking hand stretched out toward it. "Fix," the creature said, between sobs. "Somebody fix."

"Sure," Kirk said, watching intently. "We'll fix it."

The creature giggled. "Fibber," it said. The voice gradually rose to the old scream of rage. "You bustud it! Fibber, fibber!"

The clawing hand grasped the tricycle as if to use it as a weapon, but at the same time the creature seemed to catch sight of the blotches on its own naked arm. The scream died back to a whimper. "Fix it—please fix it—"

The eyes bulged, the chest heaved, and then the creature fell back to the pavement. Clearly, it was dead. McCoy knelt beside it, running a tricorder over the body.

"Impossible," he muttered.

"That it's dead?" Kirk said.

"No, that it could have lived at all. Its body temperature is over one-fifty. It must have been burning itself up. Nobody can live at that temperature."

Kirk's head snapped up suddenly. There had been another sound, coming from an alley to the left.

"Another one?" he whispered tensely. "Somebody stalking us . . . over there. Let's see if we can grab him and get some information . . . Now!"

They broke for the alley. Ahead of them they could hear the stalker running.

The alley was blind, ending in the rear of what seemed to be a small apartment house. There was no place else that the stalker could have gone. They entered cautiously, phasers ready.

The search led them eventually to what had once been a living room. There was a dusty piano in it, a child's exercise book on the music rack. Over one brittle brown page was scribbled, "Practice, practice, practice!" But there was no place to hide but a closet. Listening at the door, Kirk thought he heard agitated breathing, and then, a distinct creak. He gestured, and Spock and the security men covered him.

"Come out," he called. "We mean no harm. Come on out."

There was no answer, but the breathing was definite now. With a sudden jerk, he opened the door.

Huddled on the floor of the closet, amid heaps of moldering clothing, old shoes, a dusty umbrella, was a dark-haired young girl, no more than fourteen—probably younger. She was obviously in abject terror.

"Please," she said. "No, don't hurt me. Why did you come back?"

"We won't hurt you," Kirk said. "We want to help." He held out his hand to her, but she only tried to shrink farther back into the closet. He looked helplessly at Yeoman Rand, who came forward and knelt at the open door.

"It's all right," she said. "Nobody's going to hurt you. We promise."

"I remember the things you did," the girl said, without stirring. "Yelling, burning, hurting people."

"It wasn't us," Janice Rand said. "Come out and tell us about it."

The girl looked dubious, but allowed Janice to lead her to a chair. Clouds of dust came out of it as she sat down, still half poised to spring up and run.

"You've got a foolie," she said. "But I can't play. I don't know the rules."

"We don't either," Kirk said. "What happened to all the people? Was there a war? A plague? Did they just go someplace else and accidentally leave you here?"

"You ought to know. You did it—you and all the other grups."

"Grups? What are grups?"

The girl looked at Kirk, astonished. "You're grups. All the old ones."

"Grown-ups," Janice said. "That's what she means, Captain."

Spock, who had been moving quietly around the room with a tricorder, came back to Kirk, looking puzzled. "She can't have lived here, Captain," he said. "The dust here hasn't been disturbed for at least three hundred years, possibly longer. No radioactivity, no chemical contamination—just very old dust."

Kirk turned back to the girl. "Young lady—by the way, what's your name?"

"Miri."

"All right, Miri, you said the grups did something. Burning, hurting people. Why?"

"They did it when they started to get sick. We had to hide." She looked up hopefully at Kirk. "Am I doing it right? Is it the right foolie?"

"You're doing fine. You said the grownups got sick. Did they die?"

"Grups always die." Put that way, it was of course self-evident, but it didn't seem to advance the questioning much.

"How about the children?"

"The onlies? Of course not. We're here, aren't we?"

"More of them?" McCoy put in. "How many?"

"All there are."

"Mr. Spock," Kirk said, "take the security guards and see if you can find any more survivors ... So all the grups are gone?"

"Well, until it happens—you know—when *it* happens to an only. Then you get to be like them. You want to hurt people, like they did."

"Miri," McCoy said, "somebody attacked us, outside. You saw that? Was that a grup?"

"That was Floyd," she said, shivering a little. "It happened to him. He turned into one. It's happening to me, too. That's why I can't hang around with my friends any more. The minute one of us starts changing, the rest get afraid . . . I don't like your foolie. It's no fun."

"What do they get afraid of?" Kirk persisted.

"You saw Floyd. They try to hurt everything. First you get those awful marks on your skin. Then you turn into a grup, and you want to hurt people, kill people."

"We're not like that," Kirk said. "We've come a long way, all the way from the stars. We know a good many things. Maybe we can help you, if you'll help us."

"Grups don't help," Miri said. "They're the ones that did this."

"We didn't do it, and we want to change it. Maybe we can, if you'll trust us."

Janice touched her on the side of the face and said, "Please?" After a long moment, Miri managed her first timid smile.

Before she could speak, however, there was a prolonged rattling and clanking sound from outside, as though someone had emptied a garbage can off a rooftop. It was followed by the wasplike snarl of a phaser bolt.

Far away, and seemingly high up a child's voice called: "Nyah nyah nyah nyah. NYAH, Nyah!"

"Guards!" Spock's voice shouted.

Many voices answered, as if from all sides: "Nyah nyah nyah nyah NYAH, nyah!"

Then there was silence, except for the echoes.

"It seems," Kirk said, "that your friends don't want to be found."

"Maybe that's not the first step anyhow, Jim," McCoy said. "Whatever happened here, somewhere there must be records about it. If we're to do anything, we have to put our fingers on the cause. The best place would probably be the local public health center. What about that, Miri? Is there a place where the doctors used to work? Maybe a government building?"

"I know that place," she said distastefully. "Them and their needles. That's a bad place. None of us go there."

"But that's where we have to go," Kirk said. "It's important if we're to help you. Please take us."

He held out his hand, and, very hesitantly, she took it. She looked up at him with something like the beginnings of wonder.

"Jim is a nice name," she said. "I like it."

"I like yours, too. And I like you."

"I know you do. You can't really be a grup. You're— something different." She smiled and stood up, gracefully. As she did so, she looked down, and he felt her grip stiffen. Then, carefully, she disengaged it.

"Oh!" she said in a choked voice. "Already!"

He looked down too, already more than half aware of what he would see. Across the back of his hand was a sprawling blue blotch, about the size of a robin's egg.

The laboratory proved to be well-equipped, and since it had been sealed and was windowless, there was less than the expected coating of dust on the tables and equipment. Its size and lack of windows also made it seem unpleasantly like the inside of a tomb, but nobody was prepared to complain about that; Kirk was only grateful that its contents had proved unattractive to any looters who might have broken into it.

The blue blotches had appeared upon all of them now, although those on Mr. Spock were the smallest and appeared to spread more slowly; that was to have been expected, since he came from far different stock than did the rest of the crew, or the colonists for that matter. Just as clearly, his nonterrestrial origin conferred no immunity on him, only a slight added resistance.

McCoy had taken biopsies from the lesions; some of the samples he stained, others he cultured on a variety of media. The blood-agar plate had produced a glistening, wrinkled blue colony which turned out to consist of active, fecund bacteria strongly resembling spirochetes. McCoy, however, was convinced that these were not the cause of the disease, but only secondary invaders.

"For one thing, they won't take on any of the lab

animals I've had sent down from the ship," he said, "which means I can't satisfy Koch's Postulates. Second, there's an abnormally high number of mitotic figures in the stained tissues, and the whole appearance is about halfway between squamous metaplasia and frank neoplasm. Third, the choromosome table shows so many displacements—"

"Whoa, I'm convinced," Kirk protested. "What does it add up to?"

"I think the disease proper is caused by a virus," McCoy said. "The spirochetes may help, of course; there's an Earthly disease called Vincent's angina that's produced by two micro-organisms working in concert."

"Is the spirochete communicable?"

"Highly, by contact. You and Yeoman Rand got yours from Miri; we got them from you two."

"Then I'd better see that no one else does," Kirk said. He told his communicator: "Kirk to *Enterprise*. No one, repeat, no one, under any circumstances, is to transport down here until further notice. The planet is heavily infected. Set up complete decontamination procedures for any of us who return."

"Computer?" McCoy nudged.

"Oh yes. Also, ship us down the biggest portable bio-computer—the cat-brain job. That's to get the live-steam treatment too when it goes back up."

"Captain," Spock called. He had been going through a massed rank of file cabinets which occupied almost all of one wall. Now he was beckoning, a folder in one hand. "I think we've got something here."

They all went over except McCoy, who remained at the microscope. Spock handed the folder to Kirk and began pulling others. "There's a drawer-full of these. Must have been hundreds of people working on it. No portable bio-comp is going to process this mass of data in anything under a year."

"Then we'll feed the stuff to the ship's computer by communicator," Kirk said. He looked down at the folder.

It was headed:

Progress Report
LIFE PROLONGATION PROJECT
Genetics Section

"So *that's* what it was," Janice Rand said.

"We don't know yet," Kirk said. "But if it was. it must have been the galaxy's biggest backfire. All right, let's get to work. Miri, you can help too: lay out these folders on the long table there by categories—one for genetics, one for virology, one for immunology, or whatever. Never mind what the words mean, just match 'em up."

The picture merged with maddening slowness. The general principle was clear almost from the start: an attempt to counter the aging process by selectively repairing mutated body cells. Aging is primarily the accumulation in the body of cells whose normal functions have been partly damaged by mutations, these in turn being caused by the entrance of free radicals into the cell nucleus, thus deranging the genetic code. The colony's scientists had known very well that there was no blocking out the free radicals, which are created everywhere in the environment, by background radiation, by sunlight, by combustion, and even by digestion. Instead, they proposed to create a self-replicating, viruslike substance which would remain passive in the bloodstream until actual cell damage occurred; the virus would then penetrate the cell and replace the damaged element. The injection would be given at birth, before the baby's immunity mechanism was fully in action, so that is would be "selfed"—that is, marked as a substance normal to the body rather than an invader to be battled; but it would remain inactive until triggered by the hormones of puberty, so as not to interfere with normal growth processes.

"As bold a project as I've heard of in all my life," McCoy declared. "Just incidentally, had this thing worked, it would have been the perfect cancer preventive. Cancer is essentially just a local explosion of the aging process, in an especially virulent form."

"But it didn't work," Spock said. "Their substance was entirely *too* much like a virus—and it got away from them. Oh, it prolongs life, all right—but only in children. When puberty finally sets in, it kills them."

"How much?" Janice Rand asked.

"You mean, how long does it prolong life? We don't know because the experiment hasn't gone on that long. All we know is the rate: the injected person ages about a month, physiological time, for every hundred years, objective time. For the children, it obviously does work that way."

Janice stared at Miri. "A month in a hundred years!" she said. "And the experiment was three centuries ago! Eternal childhood...It's like a dream."

"A very bad dream, Yeoman," Kirk said. "We learn through example and responsibilities. Miri and her friends were deprived of both. It's a dead end street."

"With a particularly ugly death at the end," McCoy agreed. "It's amazing that so many children did survive. Miri, how did you get along after all the grups died?"

"We had foolies," Miri said. "We had fun. There wasn't anybody to tell us not to. And when we got hungry, we just took something. There were lots of things in cans, and lots of mommies."

"Mommies?"

"You know." Miri wound her hand vigorously in mid-air, imitating the motion of a rotary can-opener. Janice Rand choked and turned away. "Jim...now that you found what you were looking for...are you going away?"

"Oh no," Kirk said. "We've still got a great deal more to learn. Your grups seemed to have done their experiments in a certain definite sequence, a sort of timetable. Any sign of that yet, Mr. Spock?"

"No, sir. Very likely it's kept somewhere else. If this were my project, I'd keep it in a vault; it's the key to the whole business."

"I'm afraid I agree. And unless we can figure it out,

Miri, we won't be able to identify the virus, synthesize it, and make a vaccine."

"That's good," Miri said. "Your not going, I mean. We could have fun—until *it* happens."

"We still may be able to stop it. Mr. Spock, I gather you couldn't get close to any of the other children?"

"No chance. They know the area too well. Like mice."

"All right, let's try another approach. Miri, will you help us find some of them?"

"You won't find any," Miri said positively. "They're afraid. They won't like you. And they're afraid of me, too, now, ever since . . . " she stopped.

"We'll try to make them understand."

"Onlies?" the girl said. "You couldn't do it. That's the best thing about being an only. Nobody expects you to understand."

"*You* understand."

Abruptly Miri's eyes filled with tears. "I'm not an only any more," she said. She ran out of the room. Janice looked after her compassionately.

Janice said: "That little girl—"

"—is three hundred years older than you are, Yeoman," Kirk finished for her. "Don't leap to any conclusions. It's got to make some sort of a difference in her—whether we can see it yet or not."

But in a minute Miri was back, the cloudburst passed as if it had never been, looking for something to do. Mr. Spock set her to sharpening pencils, of which the ancient laboratory seemed to have scores. She set to it cheerfully—but throughout, her eyes never left Kirk. He tried not to show that he was aware of it.

"Captain? This is Farrell on the *Enterprise*. We're ready to compute."

"All right, stand by. Mr. Spock, what do you need?" Miri held up a fistful of pencils. "Are these enough?"

"Uh? Oh—we could use more, if you don't mind."

"Oh no, Jim," she said. "Why should I mind?"

"This fellow," Spock said, fanning out a sheaf of

papers on the table, "left these notes in the last weeks—after the disaster began. I disregarded these last entries; he said he was too far gone himself, too sick, to be sure he wasn't delirious, and I agree. But these earlier tables ought to show us how much time we have left. By the way, it's clear that the final stages we've seen here are typical. Homicidal mania."

"And nothing to identify the virus strain—or its chemistry?" McCoy said.

"Not a thing," Spock said. "He believed somebody else was writing that report. Maybe somebody was and we just haven't found it yet—or maybe that was the first of his hallucinations. Anyhow, the first overt stage is intense fever . . . pain in the joints . . . fuzziness of vision. Then, gradually, the mania takes over. By the way, Dr. McCoy, you were right about the spirochetes—they do contribute. They create the mania, not the virus. It'll be faster in us because we haven't carried the disease in latent form as long as Miri."

"What about her?" Kirk said in a low voice.

"Again, we'll have to see what the computer says. Roughly, I'd guess that she could survive us by five or six weeks—if one of us doesn't kill her first—"

"Enough now?" Miri said simultaneously, holding up more pencils.

"No!" Kirk burst out angrily.

The corners of her mouth turned down and her lower lip protruded. "Well, all right, Jim," she said in a small voice. "I didn't mean to make you mad."

"I'm sorry, Miri. I wasn't talking to you. I'm not mad." He turned back to Spock. "All right, so we still don't know what we're fighting. Feed your figures to Farrell and then at least we'll know what the time factor is. Damnation! If we could just put our hands on that virus, the ship could develop a vaccine for us in twenty-four hours. But there's just no starting point."

"Maybe there is," McCoy said slowly. "Again, it'd be a massive computational project, but I think it might work. Jim, you know how the desk-bound mind works.

If this lab was like every other government project I've run across, it had to have order forms in quintuplicate for everything it used. Somewhere here there ought to be an accounting file containing copies of those orders. They'd show us what the consumption of given reagents was at different times. I'll be able to spot the obvious routine items—culture media and shelf items, things like that—but we'll need to analyze for what is significant. There's at least a chance that such an analysis would reconstruct the missing timetable."

"A truly elegant idea," Mr. Spock said. "The question is—"

He was interrupted by the buzzing of Kirk's communicator.

"Kirk here."

"Farrell to landing party. Mr. Spock's table yields a cut-off point at seven days."

For a long moment there was no sound but the jerky whirring of the pencil sharpener. Then Spock said evenly:

"That was the question I was about to raise. As much as I admire Dr. McCoy's scheme, it will almost surely require more time than we have left."

"Not necessarily," McCoy said. "If it's true that the spirochete creates the mania, we can possibly knock it out with antibiotics and keep our minds clear for at least a while longer—"

Something hit the floor with a smash. Kirk whirled. Janice Rand had been cleaning some of McCoy's slides in a beaker of chromic acid. The corrosive yellow stuff was now all over the floor. Some of it had spattered Janice's legs. Grabbing a wad of cotton, Kirk dropped to his knees to mop them.

"No, no," Janice sobbed. "You can't help me—you can't help me!"

Stumbling past McCoy and Spock, she ran out of the laboratory, sobbing. Kirk started after her.

"Stay here," he said. "Keep working. Don't lose a minute."

Janice was standing in the hallway, her back turned,

weeping convulsively. Kirk resumed swabbing her legs, trying not to notice the ugly blue blotches marring them. As he worked, her tears gradually died back. After a while she said in a small voice:

"Back on the ship you never noticed my legs."

Kirk forced a chuckle. "The burden of command, Yeoman: to see only what regs say is pertinent... That's better, but soap and water will have to be next."

He stood up. She looked worn, but no longer hysterical. She said:

"Captain, I didn't really want to do that."

"I know," Kirk said. "Forget it."

"It's so stupid, such a waste... Sir, do you know all I can think about? I should know better, but I keep thinking, I'm only twenty-four—and I'm scared."

"I'm a little older, Yeoman. But I'm scared too."

"You are?"

"Of course. I don't want to become one of those things, any more than you do. I'm more than scared. You're my people. I brought you here. I'm scared for all of us."

"You don't show it," she whispered. "You never show it. You always seem to be braver than any ten of us."

"Baloney," he said roughly. "Only an idiot isn't afraid when there's something to be afraid of. The man who feels no fear isn't brave, he's just stupid. Where courage comes in is in going ahead and coping with danger, not being paralyzed by fright. And especially, not letting yourself be panicked by the other guy."

"I draw the moral," Janice said, trying to pull herself erect. But at the same time, the tears started coming quietly again. "I'm sorry," she repeated in a strained voice. "When we get back, sir, you'd better put in for a dry-eyed Yeoman."

"Your application for a transfer is refused." He put his arm around her gently, and she tried to smile up at him. The movement turned them both around toward the entrance to the lab.

Standing in it was Miri, staring at them with her

fists crammed into her mouth, her eyes wide with an unfathomable mixture of emotions—amazement, protest, hatred even? Kirk could not tell. As he started to speak, Miri whirled about and was gone. He could hear her running footsteps receding; then silence.

"Troubles never come alone," Kirk said resignedly. "We'd better go back."

"Where was Miri going?" McCoy asked interestedly, the moment they re-entered. "She seemed to be in a hurry."

"I don't know. Maybe to try and look for more onlies. Or maybe she just got bored with us. We haven't time to worry about her. What's next?"

"Next is accident prevention time," McCoy said. "I should have thought of it before, but Janice's accident reminded me of it. There are a lot of corrosive reagents around here, and if we have any luck, we'll soon be playing with infectious material too. I want everyone out of their regular clothes and into lab uniforms we can shuck the minute they get something spilled on them. There's a whole locker full of them over on that side. All our own clothes go out of the lab proper into the anteroom, or else we'll just have to burn 'em when we get back to the ship."

"Good; so ordered. How about equipment—phasers and so on?"

"Keep one phaser here for emergencies if you're prepared to jettison it before we go back," McCoy said. "Everything else, out."

"Right. Next?"

"Medical analysis has got as far as I can take it," McCoy said. "From here on out, it's going to be strictly statistical—and though the idea was mine, I'm afraid Mr. Spock is going to have to direct it. Statistics make me gibber."

Kirk grinned. "Very well, Mr. Spock, take over."

"Yes sir. First of all, we've got to find those purchase orders. Which means another search of the file cabinets."

The problem was simple to pose: Invent a disease.

The accounting records turned up, relatively promptly, and in great detail. McCoy's assumption had been right that far: the bureaucratic mind evidently underwent no substantial change simply by having been removed more than a dozen light-years from the planet where it had evolved. Everything the laboratory had ever had to call for had at least three pieces of paper that went along with it.

McCoy was able to sort these into rough categories of significance, on a scale of ten (from 0 = obvious nonsense to 10 = obviously crucial), and the bio-comp coded everything graded "five" or above so that it could be fed to the orbiting *Enterprise's* computer with the least possible loss of time. The coding was very fast; but assigning relative weights to the items to be coded was a matter for human judgment, and despite his disclaimers, McCoy was the only man present who could do it with any confidence in well more than half of the instances. Spock could tell, within a given run of samples, what appeared to be statistically significant, but only McCoy could then guess whether the associations were medical, financial, or just make-work.

It took two days, working around the clock. By the morning of the third day, however, Spock was able to say:

"These cards now hold everything the bio-comp can do for us." He turned to Miri, who had returned the day before, with no explanations, but without the slightest change in her manner, and as willing to work as ever. "Miri, if you'll just stack them and put them back in that hopper, we'll rank them for the *Enterprise*, and then we can read-and-feed to Farrell. I must confess, I still don't see the faintest trace of a pattern in them."

"I do," McCoy said surprisingly. "Clearly the active agent can't be a pure virus, because it'd be cleaned out of the body between injection and puberty if it didn't reproduce; and true viruses can't reproduce without invading a body cell, which this thing is forbidden to do for some ten or twelve years, depending on the sex of the host. This has to be something more like some of the rickettsiae, with some enyzmatic mechanisms intact so it can feed and reproduce from material it can absorb from the body fluids, *outside* the cells. When the hormones of puberty hit it, it sheds that part of its organization and becomes a true virus. Ergo, the jettisoned mechanism has to be steroid-soluble. And only the sexual steroids can be involved. All these conditions close in on it pretty implacably, step by step."

"Close enough to put a name to it?" Kirk demanded tensely.

"By no means," McCoy said. "I don't even know if I'm on the right track; this whole scholium is intuitive on my part. But it makes sense. I think something very like that will emerge when the ship's computer processes all these codes. Anybody care to bet?"

"We've already bet our lives, like it or not," Kirk said. "But we ought to have the answer in an hour now. Mr. Spock, call Farrell."

Spock nodded and went out into the anteroom, now kept sealed off from the rest of the lab. He was back in a moment. Though his face was almost incapable of showing emotion, something in his look brought Kirk to his feet in a rush.

"What's the matter?"

"The communicators are gone, Captain. There's nothing in those uniforms but empty pockets."

Janice gasped. Kirk turned to Miri, feeling his brows knotting together. The girl shrank a little from him, but returned his look defiantly all the same.

"What do you know about this, Miri?"

"The onlies took them, I guess," she said. "They like to steal things. It's a foolie."

"Where did they take them?"

She shrugged. "I don't know. That's a foolie, too. When you take something, you go someplace else."

He was on her in two strides, grasping her by the

shoulders. "This is not a foolie. It's a disaster. We have to have those communicators—otherwise we'll never lick this disease."

She giggled suddenly. "Then you won't have to go," she said.

"No, we'll die. Now cut it out. Tell us where they are."

The girl drew herself up in an imitation of adult dignity. Considering that she had never seen an adult after the disaster until less than a week ago, it was a rather creditable imitation.

"Please, Captain, you're hurting me," she said haughtily. "What's the matter with you? How could *I* possibly know?"

Unfortunately, the impersonation broke at the end into another giggle—which, however, did Kirk no good as far as the issue at hand was concerned. "What is this, blackmail?" Kirk said, beyond anger now. He could feel nothing but the total urgency of the loss. "It's your life that's at stake too, Miri."

"Oh no," Miri said sweetly. "Mr. Spock said that I'd live five or six weeks longer than you will. Maybe some of you'll die ahead of some others. I'll still be here." She flounced in her rags toward the door. Under any other circumstances she might have been funny, perhaps even charming. At the last moment she turned, trailing a languid hand through the air. "Of course I don't know what makes you think I know anything about this. But maybe if you're very nice to me, I could ask my friends some questions. In the meantime, Captain, farewell."

There was an explosion of pent breaths as her footsteps dwindled.

"Well," McCoy said, "one can tell that they had television on this planet during part of Miri's lifetime, at least."

The grim joke broke part of the tension.

"What can we do without the ship?" Kirk demanded. "Mr. Spock?"

"Very little, Captain. The bio-comp's totally inadequate

for this kind of job. It takes hours, where the ship's computer takes seconds, and it hasn't the analytical capacity."

"The human brain was around long before there were computers. Bones, what about your hunch?"

"I'll ride it, of course," McCoy said wearily. "But time is the one commodity the computer could have saved us, and the one thing we haven't got. When I think of that big lumbering ship up there, with everything we need on board it, orbiting around and around like so much inert metal—"

"And complaining just wastes more time," Kirk snarled. McCoy stared at him in surprise. "I'm sorry, Bones. I guess it's starting to get me, too."

"I *was* complaining," McCoy said. "The apology is mine. Well then, the human brain it will have to be. It worked for Pasteur . . . but he was a good bit smarter than me. Mr. Spock, take those cards away from that dumb cat and let's restack them. I'll want to try a DNA analysis first. If that makes any sort of reasonable pattern, enough to set up a plausible species, we'll chew through them again and see if we can select out a clone."

"I'm not following you," Spock admitted.

"I'll feed you the codes, there's no time for explanations. Pull everything coded LTS-426 first. Then we'll ask the cat to sort those for uncoded common factors. There probably won't be any, but it's the most promising beginning I can think of."

"Right."

Kirk felt even more out of it than Mr. Spock; he had neither the medical nor the statistical background to understand what was going on. He simply stood by, and did what little donkey-work there was to do.

The hours wore away into another day. Despite the stim-pills McCoy doled out, everyone seemed to be moving very slowly, as if underwater. It was like a nightmare of flight.

Somewhere during that day, Miri turned up, to watch with what she probably imagined was an expression of aloof amusement. Everyone ignored her. The expression gradually faded into a frown; finally, she began to tap her foot.

"Stop that," Kirk said without even turning to look at her, "or I'll break your infant neck."

The tapping stopped. McCoy said: "Once more into the cat, Mr. Spock. We are now pulling all T's that are functions of D-2. If there are more than three, we're sunk."

The bio-comp hummed and chuttered over the twenty-two cards Spock had fed it. It threw out just one. McCoy leaned back in his hard-backed straight chair with a whoosh of satisfaction.

"Is that it?" Kirk asked.

"By no means, Jim. That's *probably* the virus involved. Just probably, no more."

"It's only barely significant," Spock said. "If this were a test on a new product survey or something of that sort, I'd throw it out without a second thought. But as matters stand—"

"As matters stand, we next have to synthesize the virus," McCoy said, "and then make a killed-virus vaccine from it. No, no, that won't work at all, what's the matter with me? Not a vaccine. An antitoxoid. Much harder. Jim, wake those security guards—a lot of good they did us in the pinch! We are going to need a lot of bottles washed in the next forty-eight hours."

Kirk wiped his forehead. "Bones, I'm feeling outright lousy, and I'm sure you are too. Officially we've got the forty-eight hours left—but are we going to be functioning sensibly after the next twenty-four?"

"We either fish or cut bait," McCoy said calmly. "All hands on their feet. The cookery class is hereby called to order."

"It's a shame," Spock said, "that viruses aren't as easy to mix as metaphors."

At this point Kirk knew that he was on the thin edge of hysteria. Somehow he had the firm impression that Mr. Spock had just made a joke. Next he would be beginning to believe that there really was such a thing as a portable computer with a cat's brain in it. "Somebody hand me a bottle to wash," he said, "before I go to sleep on my feet."

By the end of twenty hours, Janice Rand was raving and had to be strapped down and given a colossal tranquilizer dose before she would stop fighting. One of the guards followed her down an hour later. Both were nearly solid masses of blue marks; evidently, the madness grew as the individual splotches coalesced into larger masses and proceeded toward covering the whole skin surface.

Miri disappeared at intervals, but she manag d to be n the scene for both these collapses. Perhaps she was trying to look knowing, or superior, or amused; Kirk could not tell. The fact of the matter was that he no longer had to work to ignore Miri, he was so exhausted that the small chores allotted him by his First Officer and his ship's surgeon took up the whole foreground of his attention, and left room for no background at all.

Somewhere in there, McCoy's voice said: "Everything under the SPF hood now. At the next stage we've got a live one. Kirk, when I take the lid off the Petri dish, in goes the two cc's of formalin. Don't miss."

"I won't."

Somehow, he didn't. Next, after a long blank, he was looking at a rubber-capped ampule filled with clear liquid, into which McCoy's hands were inserting the needle of a spray hypo. Tunnel vision; nothing more than that: the ampule, the hypo, the hands.

"That's either the antitoxoid," McCoy's voice was saying from an infinite distance, "or it isn't. For all I know it may be pure poison. Only the computer could tell us which for sure."

"Janice first," Kirk heard himself rasp. "Then the guard. They're the closest to terminal."

"I override you, Captain," McCoy's voice said. "I am the only experimental animal in this party."

The needle jerked out of the rubber cap. Somehow, Kirk managed to reach out and grasp McCoy's only visible wrist. The movement hurt; his joints ached abominably, and so did his head.

"Wait a minute," he said. "One minute more won't make any difference."

He swivelled his ringing skull until Miri came into view down the optical tunnel. She seemed to be all fuzzed out at the edges. Kirk walked toward her, planting his feet with extraordinary care on the slowly tilting floor.

"Miri," he said. "Listen to me. You've got to listen to me."

She turned her head away. He reached out and grabbed her by the chin, much more roughly than he had wanted to, and forced her to look at him. He was dimly aware that he was anything but pretty—bearded, covered with sweat and dirt, eyes rimmed and netted with red, mouth working with the effort to say words that would not come out straight.

"We've . . . only got a few hours left. Us, and all of you . . . you, and your friends. And . . . we may be wrong. After that, no grups, and no onlies . . . no one . . . forever and ever. Give me back just one of those . . . machines, those communicators. Do you want the blood of a whole world on your hands? Think, Miri—think for once in your life!"

Her eyes darted away. She was looking toward Janice. He forced her to look back at him. "Now, Miri. Now. *Now*."

She drew a long, shuddering breath. "I'll—try to get you one," she said. Then she twisted out of his grasp and vanished.

"We can't wait any longer," McCoy's voice said calmly. "Even if we had the computer's verdict, we couldn't do anything with it. We have to go ahead."

"I will bet you a year's pay," Spock said, "that the antitoxoid is fatal in itself."

In a haze of pain, Kirk could see McCoy grinning tightly, like a skull. "You're on," he said. "The disease certainly is. But if I lose, Mr. Spock, how will you collect?"

He raised his hand.

"Stop!" Kirk croaked. He was too late—even supposing that McCoy in this last extremity would have obeyed his captain. This was McCoy's world, his universe of discourse. The hypo hissed against the surgeon's bared, blue-suffused arm.

Calmly, McCoy laid the injector down on the table, and sat down. "Done," he said. "I don't feel a thing." His eyes rolled upward in their sockets, and he took a firm hold on the edge of the table. "You see ... gentlemen ... it's all perfectly ... "

His head fell forward.

"Help me carry him," Kirk said, in a dead voice. Together, he and Spock carried the surgeon to the nearest cot. McCoy's face, except for the botches, was waxlike; he looked peaceful for the first time in days. Kirk sat down on the edge of the cot beside him and tried his pulse. It was wild and erratic, but still there.

"I ... don't see how the antitoxoid could have hit him that fast," Spock said. His own voice sounded like a whisper from beyond the grave.

"He could only have passed out. I'm about ready, myself. Damn the man's stubbornness."

"Knowledge," Spock said remotely, "has its privileges."

This meant nothing to Kirk. Spock was full of these gnomic utterances; presumably they were Vulcanian. There was a peculiar hubbub in Kirk's ears, as though the visual fuzziness was about to be counterpointed by an aural one.

Spock said, "I seem to be on the verge myself—closer than I thought. The hallucinations have begun."

Wearily, Kirk looked around. Then he goggled. If Spock was having a hallucination, so was Kirk. He wondered if it was the same one.

A procession of children was coming into the room, led by Miri. They were of all sizes and shapes, from toddlers up to about the age of twelve. They looked as though they had been living in a department store. Some of the older boys wore tuxedos; some were in military uniforms; some in scaled-down starmen's clothes; some in very loud and mismatched sports clothes. The girls were a somewhat better matched lot, since almost all of them were wearing some form of party dress, several of them trailing opera cloaks and loaded with jewelry. Dominating them all was a tall, red-headed boy—or no, that wasn't his own hair, it was a wig, long at the back and sides and with bangs, from which the price-tag still dangled. Behind him hopped a fat little boy who was carrying, on a velvet throw-pillow, what appeared to be a crown.

It was like some mad vision of the Children's Crusade. But what was maddest about it was that the children were loaded with equipment—the landing party's equipment. There were the three communicators—Janice and the security guards hadn't carried any; there were the two missing tricorders—McCoy had kept his in the lab; and the red-wigged boy even had a phaser slung at his hip. It was a measure of how exhausted they had all been, even back then, that they hadn't realized one of the deadly objects was missing. Kirk wondered whether the boy had tried it, and if so, whether he had hurt anybody with it.

The boy saw him looking at it, and somehow divined his thought.

"I used it on Louise," he said gravely. "I had to. She went grup all at once, while we were playing school. She was—only a little older than me."

He unbuckled the weapon and held it out. Numbly, Kirk took it. The other children moved to the long table and solemnly began to pile the rest of the equipment on it. Miri came tentatively to Kirk.

"I'm sorry," she said. "It was wrong and I shouldn't have. I had a hard time, trying to make Jahn understand that it wasn't a foolie any more." She looked sideways at the waxy figure of McCoy. "Is it too late?"

"It may be," Kirk whispered; that was all the voice he could muster. "Mr. Spock, do you think you can still read the data to Farrell?"

"I'll try, sir."

Farrell was astonished and relieved, and demanded explanations. Spock cut him short and read him the figures. Then there was nothing to do but wait while the material was processed. Kirk went back to looking at McCoy, and Miri joined him. He realized dimly that, for all the trouble she had caused, her decision to bring the communicators back had been a giant step toward growing up. It would be a shame to lose her now, Miri most of all in the springtime of her promise—a springtime for which she had waited three sordid centuries. He put his arm around her, and she looked up at him gratefully.

Was it another failure of vision, or were the blotches on McCoy fading a little? No, some of them were definitely smaller and had lost color. "Mr. Spock," he said, "come here and check me on something."

Spock looked and nodded. "Retreating," he said. "Now if there are no serious side-effects—" The buzz of his communicator interrupted him. "Spock here."

"Farrell to landing party. The identification is correct, repeat, correct. Congratulations. Do you mean to tell me you boiled down all that mass of bits and pieces with nothing but a bio-comp?"

Kirk and Spock exchanged tired grins. "No," Spock said, "we did it all in Doctor McCoy's head. Over and out."

"The bio-comp did help," Kirk said. He reached out and patted the squat machine. "Nice kitty."

McCoy stirred. He was trying to sit up, his expression dazed.

"Begging your pardon, Doctor," Kirk said. "If you've rested sufficently, I believe the administration of injections *is* your department."

"It worked?" McCoy said huskily.

"It worked fine, the ship's computer says it's the right stuff, and you are the hero of the hour, you pig-headed idiot."

They left the system a week later, having given all the antitoxoid the ship's resources could produce. Together with Farrell, the erstwhile landing party stood on the bridge of the *Enterprise*, watching the planet retreat.

"I'm still a little uneasy about it," Janice Rand said. "No matter how old they are chronologically, they're still just children. And to leave them there with just a medical team to help them—"

"They haven't lived all those years for nothing," Kirk said. "Look at the difficult thing Miri did. They'll catch on fast, with only a minimum of guidance. Besides, I've already had Lieutenant Uhura get the word back to Earth... If that planet had had subspace radio, they would have been saved a lot of their agony. But it hadn't been invented when the original colonists left... Space Central will send teachers, technicians, administrators—"

"—And truant officers, I presume," McCoy said.

"No doubt. The kids will be all right."

Janice Rand said slowly: "Miri... she... really loved you, you know, Captain. That was why she played that trick on you."

"I know," Kirk said. "And I'm duly flattered. But I'll tell you a secret, Yeoman Rand. I make it a policy never to get involved with women older than I am."

The Conscience of the King

᙮᙮

"A curious experience," Kirk said. "I've seen *Macbeth* in everything from bearskins to uniforms, but never before in Arcturian dress. I suppose an actor has to adapt to all kinds of audiences."

"This one has," Dr. Leighton said. He exchanged a glance with Martha Leighton; there was an undertone in his voice which Kirk could not fathom. There seemed to be no reason for it. The Leightons' garden, under the bright sun of the Arcturian system, was warm and pleasant; their hospitality, including last night's play, had been unexceptionable. But time was passing, and old friends or no, Kirk had to be back on duty shortly.

"Karidian has an enormous reputation," he said, "and obviously he's earned it. But now, Tom, we'd better get down to business. I've been told this new synthetic of yours is something we badly need."

"There is no synthetic," Leighton said heavily. "I want you to think about Karidian. About his voice in particular. You should remember it; you were there."

"I was where?" Kirk said, annoyed. "At the play?"

"No," Leighton said, his crippled, hunched body stirring restlessly in its lounger. "On Tarsus IV, during the Rebellion. Of course it was twenty years ago, but you

118

couldn't have forgotten. My family murdered—and your friends. And you saw Kodos—and heard him, too."

"Do you mean to tell me," Kirk said slowly, "that you called me three light-years off my course just to accuse an actor of being Kodos the Executioner? What am I supposed to put in my log? That you lied? That you diverted a starship with false information?"

"It's not false. Karidian is Kodos."

"That's not what I'm talking about. I'm talking about your invented story about the synthetic food process. Anyhow, Kodos is dead."

"Is he?" Leighton said. "A body burned beyond recognition—what kind of evidence is that? And there are so few witnesses left, Jim: you, and I, and perhaps six or seven others, people who actually saw Kodos and heard his voice. You may have forgotten, but I never will."

Kirk turned to Martha, but she said gently: "I can't tell him anything, Jim. Once he heard Karidian's voice, it all came back. I can hardly blame him. From all accounts, that was a bloody business . . . and Tom wasn't just a witness. He was a victim."

"No, I know that," Kirk said. "But vengeance won't help, either—and I can't allow the whole *Enterprise* to be sidetracked on a personal vendetta, no matter how I feel about it."

"And what about justice?" Leighton said. "If Kodos is still alive, oughtn't he to pay? Or at least be taken out of circulation—before he contrives another massacre? Four thousand people, Jim!"

"You have a point," Kirk admitted reluctantly. "All right, I'll go this far: Let me check the ship's library computer and see what we have on *both* men. If your notion's just a wild hare, that's probably the quickest way to find out. If it isn't—well, I'll listen further."

"Fair enough," Leighton said.

Kirk pulled out his communicator and called the *Enterprise*. "Library computer . . . Give me everything you have on a man named or known as Kodos the

Executioner. After that, a check on an actor named Anton Karidian."

"Working," the computer's voice said. Then: "Kodos the Executioner. Deputy Commander, forces of Rebellion, Tarsus IV, twenty terrestrial years ago. Population of eight thousand Earth colonists struck by famine after fungus blight largely destroyed food supply. Kodos used situation to implement private theories of eugenics, slaughtered fifty per cent of colony population. Sought by Earth forces when rebellion overcome. Burned body found and case closed. Biographical data—"

"Skip that," Kirk said. "Go on."

"Karidian, Anton. Director and leading man of traveling company of actors, sponsored by Interstellar Cultural Exchange project. Touring official installations for past nine years. Daughter, Lenore, nineteen years old, now leading lady of troupe. Karidian a recluse, has given notice current tour is to be his last. Credits—"

"Skip that too. Data on his pre-acting years?"

"None available. That is total information."

Kirk put the communicator away slowly. "Well, well," he said. "I still think it's probably a wild hare, Tom . . . but I think I'd better go to tonight's performance, too."

After the performance, Kirk went backstage, which was dingy and traditional, and knocked on the door with the star on it. In a moment, Lenore Karidian opened it, still beautiful, though not as bizarre as she had looked as an Arcturian Lady Macbeth. She raised her eyebrows.

"I saw your performance tonight," Kirk said. "And last night, too. I just want to . . . extend my appreciation to you and to Karidian."

"Thank you," she said, politely. "My father will be delighted, Mr. . . .?"

"Capt. James Kirk, the starship *Enterprise*."

That told, he could tell; that and the fact that he had seen the show two nights running. She said: "We're honored. I'll carry your message to father."

"Can't I see him personally?"

"I'm sorry, Captain Kirk. He sees no one personally."

"An actor turning away his admirers? That's very unusual."

"Karidian is an unusual man."

"Then I'll talk with Lady Macbeth," Kirk said. "If you've no objections. May I come in?"

"Why . . . of course." She moved out of the way. Inside, the dressing room was a clutter of theatrical trunks, all packed and ready to be moved. "I'm sorry I have nothing to offer you."

Kirk stared directly at her, smiling. "You're being unnecessarily modest."

She smiled back. "As you see, everything is packed. Next we play two performances on Benecia, if the *Astral Queen* can get us there; we leave tonight."

"She's a good ship," Kirk said. "Do you enjoy your work?"

"Mostly. But, to play the classics, in these times, when most people prefer absurd three-V serials . . . it isn't always as rewarding as it could be."

"But you continue," Kirk said.

"Oh yes," she said, with what seemed to be a trace of bitterness. "My father feels that we owe it to the public. Not that the public cares."

"They cared tonight. You were very convincing as Lady Macbeth."

"Thank you. And as Lenore Karidian?"

"I'm impressed." He paused an instant. "I think I'd like to see you again."

"Professionally?"

"Not necessarily."

"I . . . think I'd like that. Unfortunately, we must keep to our schedule."

"Schedules aren't always as rigid as they seem," Kirk said. "Shall we see what happens?"

"Very well. And hope for the best."

The response was promising, if ambiguous, but Kirk had no chance to explore it further. Suddenly his communicator was beeping insistently.

"Excuse me," he said. "That's my ship calling . . . Kirk here."

"Spock calling, Captain. Something I felt you should know immediately. Dr. Leighton is dead."

"Dead? Are you sure?"

"Absolutely," Spock's voice said. "We just had word from Q Central. He was murdered—stabbed to death."

Slowly, Kirk put the device back in his hip pocket. Lenore was watching him. Her face showed nothing but grave sympathy.

"I'll have to go," he said. "Perhaps you'll hear from me later."

"I quite understand. I hope so."

Kirk went directly to the Leightons' apartment. The body was still there, unattended except by Martha, but it told him nothing; he was not an expert in such matters. He took Martha's hand gently.

"He really died the first day those players arrived," she said, very quietly. "Memory killed him. Jim . . . do you suppose survivors ever really recover from a tragedy?"

"I'm deeply sorry, Martha."

"He was convinced the moment we saw that man arrive," she said. "Twenty years since the terror, but he was sure Karidian was the man. Is that possible, Jim? Is he Kodos, after all?"

"I don't know. But I'm trying to find out."

"Twenty years and he still had nightmares. I'd wake him and he'd tell me he still heard the screams of the innocent—the silence of the executed. They never told him what happened to the rest of his family."

"I'm afraid there's not much doubt about that," Kirk said.

"It's the not knowing, Jim—whether the people you love are dead or alive. When you know, you mourn, but the wound heals and you go on. When you don't— every dawn is a funeral. That's what killed my husband, Jim, not the knife . . . But with him, I know."

She managed a small smile and Kirk squeezed her

hand convulsively. "It's all right," she said, as if she were the one who had to do the comforting. "At least he has peace now. He never really had it before. I suppose we'll never know who killed him."

"I," Kirk said, "am damn well going to find out."

"It doesn't matter. I've had enough of all this passion for vengeance. It's time to let it all rest. More than time."

Suddenly the tears welled up. "But I shan't forget him. Never."

Kirk stomped aboard ship in so obvious a white fury that nobody dared even to speak to him. Going directly to his quarters, he barked into the intercom: "Uhura!"

"Yes, Captain," the Communications Officer responded, her normally firm voice softened almost to a squeak.

"Put me through to Captain Daly, the *Astral Queen,* on orbit station. And put it on scramble."

"Yes, *sir* . . . He's on, sir."

"John, this is Jim Kirk. Can you do me a little favor?"

"I owe you a dozen," Daly's voice said. "And two dozen drinks, too. Name your poison."

"Thanks. I want you to pass up your pickup here."

"You mean strand all them actors?"

"Just that," Kirk said. "I'll take them on. And if there's any trouble, the responsibility is mine."

"Will do."

"I appreciate it. I'll explain later—I hope. Over and out . . . Lieutenant Uhura, now I want the library computer."

"Library."

"Reference the Kodos file. I'm told there were eight or nine survivors of the massacre who were actual eyewitnesses. I want their names and status."

"Working . . . In order of age: Leighton, T., deceased. Molson, E., deceased—"

"Wait a minute, I want survivors."

"These were survivors of the massacre," the computer said primly. "The deceased are all recent murder victims, all cases open. Instructions."

Kirk swallowed. "Continue."

"Kirk, J., Captain, S.S. *Enterprise*. Wiegand, R., deceased. Eames, S., deceased. Daiken, R. Communications, S.S. *Enterprise*—"

"What!"

"Daiken, R., Communications, *Enterprise,* five years old at time of Kodos incident."

"All right, cut," Kirk said. "Uhura, get me Mr. Spock ... Mr. Spock, arrange for a pickup for the Karidian troupe, to be recorded in the log as stranded, for transfer to their destination; company to present special performance for officers and crew. Next destination to be Eta Benecia; give me arrival time as soon as it's processed."

"Aye, aye, sir. What about the synthetic food samples we were supposed to pick up from Dr. Leighton?"

"There aren't any, Mr. Spock," Kirk said shortly.

"That fact will have to be noted, too. Diverting a starship—"

"Is a serious business. Well, a black mark against Dr. Leighton isn't going to hurt him now. One more thing, Mr. Spock. I want the privacy of the Karidian company totally respected. They can have the freedom of the ship within the limits of regulations, but their quarters are off limits. Pass it on to all hands."

"Yes, sir." There was no emotion in Spock's voice; but then, there never was.

"Finally, Mr. Spock, reference Lt. Robert Daiken, in Communications. Please have him transferred to Engineering."

"Sir," Spock said, "he came up from Engineering."

"I'm aware of that. I'm sending him back. He needs more experience."

"Sir, may I suggest a further explanation? He's bound to consider this transfer a disciplinary action."

"I can't help that," Kirk said curtly. "Execute. And notify me when the Karidians come aboard."

He paused and looked up at the ceiling, at last unable to resist a rather grim smile. "I think," he said, "I shall be taking the young lady on a guided tour of the ship."

There was quite a long silence. Then Spock said neutrally:

"As you wish, sir."

At this hour, the engine room was empty, and silent except for the low throbbing of the great thrust units; the *Enterprise* was driving. Lenore looked around, and then smiled at Kirk.

"Did you order the soft lights especially for the occasion?" she said.

"I'd like to be able to say yes," Kirk said. "However, we try to duplicate conditions of night and day as much as possible. Human beings have a built-in diurnal rhythm; we try to adjust to it." He gestured at the hulking drivers. "You find this interesting?"

"Oh yes . . . All that power, and all under such complete control. Are you like that, Captain?"

"I hope I'm more of a man than a machine," he said.

"An intriguing combination of both. The power's at your command; but the decisions—"

"—come from a very human source."

"Are you sure?" she said. "Exceptional, yes; but human?"

Kirk said softly, "You can count on it."

There was a sound of footsteps behind them. Kirk turned reluctantly. It was Yeoman Rand, looking in this light peculiarly soft and blonde despite her uniform—and despite a rather severe expression. She held out an envelope.

"Excuse me, sir," she said. "Mr. Spock thought you ought to have this at once."

"Quite so. Thank you." Kirk pocketed the envelope. "That will be all."

"Very good, sir." The girl left without batting an eyelash. Lenore watched her go, seemingly somewhat amused.

"A lovely girl," she said.

"And very efficient."

"Now *there's* a subject, Captain. Tell me about the

women in your world. Has the machine changed them? Made them, well, just people, instead of women?"

"Not at all," Kirk said. "On this ship they have the same duties and functions as the men. They compete equally, and get no special privileges. But they're still women."

"I can see that. Especially the one who just left. So pretty. I'm afraid she didn't like me."

"Nonsense," Kirk said, rather more bluffly than he had intended. "You're imagining things. Yeoman Rand is all business."

Lenore looked down. "You are human, after all. Captain of a starship, and yet you know so little about women. Still I can hardly blame her."

"Human nature hasn't changed," Kirk said. "Grown, perhaps, expanded . . . but not changed."

"That's a comfort. To know that people can still feel, build a private dream, fall in love . . . all that, and power too! Like Caesar—and Cleopatra."

She was moving steadily closer, by very small degrees. Kirk waited a moment, and then took her in his arms.

The kiss was warm and lingering. She was the first to draw out of it, looking up into his eyes, her expression half sultry, half mocking.

"I had to know," she whispered against the power hum. "I never kissed a Caesar before."

"A rehearsal, Miss Karidian?"

"A performance, Captain."

They kissed again, hard. Something crackled against Kirk's breast. After what seemed to be all too short a while, he took her by the shoulders and pushed her gently away—not very far.

"Don't stop."

"I'm not stopping, Lenore. But I'd better see what it was that Spock thought was so important. He had orders not to know where I was."

"I see," she said, her voice taking on a slight edge. "Starship captains tell *before* they kiss. Well, go ahead and look at your note."

Kirk pulled out the envelope and ripped it open. The message was brief, pointed, very Spock-like. It said:

SHIP'S OFFICER DAIKEN POISONED, CONDITION SERIOUS. DR. McCOY ANALYZING FOR CAUSE AND ANTIDOTE, REQUESTS YOUR PRESENCE.
SPOCK

Lenore watched his face change. At last she said, "I see I've lost you. I hope not permanently."

"No, hardly permanently," Kirk said, trying to smile and failing. "But I should have looked at this sooner. Excuse me, please; and goodnight, Lady Macbeth."

Spock and McCoy were in the sick bay when Kirk arrived. Daiken was on the table, leads running from his still, sweating form to the body function panel, which seemed to be quietly going crazy. Kirk flashed a glance over the panel, but it meant very little to him. He said: "Will he make it? What happened?"

"Somebody put tetralubisol in his milk," McCoy said. "A clumsy job; the stuff is poisonous, but almost insoluble, so it was easy to pump out. He's sick, but he has a good chance. More than I can say for you, Jim."

Kirk looked sharply at the surgeon, and then at Spock. They were both watching him like cats.

"Very well," he said. "I can see that I'm on the spot. Mr. Spock, why don't you begin the lecture?"

"Daiken was the next to last witness of the Kodos affair," Spock said evenly. "You are the last. Dr. McCoy and I checked the library, just as you did, and got the same information. We suppose you are courting Miss Karidian for more information—but the next attempt will be on you. Clearly, you and Daiken are the only survivors because you are both aboard the *Enterprise*; but if Dr. Leighton was right, you no longer have that immunity, and the attempt on Daiken tends to confirm that. In short, you're inviting death."

"I've done that before," Kirk said tiredly. "If Karidian is Kodos, I mean to nail him down, that's all. Administering justice is part of my job."

"Are you certain that's all?" McCoy said.

"No, Bones, I'm not at all certain. Remember that I was there on Tarsus—a midshipman, caught up in a revolution. I saw women and children forced into a chamber with no exit ... and a half-mad self-appointed messiah named Kodos throw a switch. And then there wasn't anyone inside any more. Four thousand people, dead, vanished—and I had to stand by, just waiting for my own turn ... I can't forget it, any more than Leighton could. I thought I had, but I was wrong."

"And what if you decide Karidian is Kodos?" McCoy demanded. "What then? Do you carry his head through the corridors in triumph? That won't bring back the dead."

"Of course it won't," Kirk said. "But they may rest easier."

"Vengeance is mine, saith the Lord," Spock said, almost in a whisper. Both men turned to look at him in astonishment

At last Kirk said, "That's true, Mr. Spock, whatever it may mean to an outworlder like you. Vengeance is not what I'm after. I am after justice—and prevention. Kodos killed four thousand; if he is still at large, he may massacre again. But consider this, too: Karidian is a human being, with rights like all of us. He deserves the same justice. If it's at all possible, he also deserves to be cleared."

"I don't know who's worse," McCoy said, looking from Spock to Kirk, "the human calculator or the captain-cum-mystic. Both of you go the hell away and leave me with my patient."

"Gladly," Kirk said. "I'm going to talk to Karidian, and never mind his rule against personal interviews. He can try to kill me if he likes, but he'll have to lay off my officers."

"In short," Spock said, "you *do* think Karidian is Kodos."

Kirk threw up his hands. "Of course I do, Mr. Spock," he said. "Would I be making such an idiot of myself if I didn't? But I am going to make sure. That's the only definition of justice that I know."

"I," Spock said, "would have called it logic."

Karidian and his daughter were not only awake when they answered Kirk's knock, but already half in costume for the next night's command performance which was part of the official excuse for their being on board the *Enterprise* at all. Karidian was wearing a dressing-gown which might have been the robe of Hamlet, the ghost, or the murderer king; whichever it was, he looked kingly, an impression which he promptly reinforced by crossing to a tall-backed chair and sitting down in it as if it were a throne. In his lap he held a much-worn prompter's copy of the play, with his name scrawled across it by a felt pen.

Lenore was easier to tape: she was the mad Ophelia . . . or else, simply a nineteen-year-old girl in a nightgown. Karidian waved her into the background. She withdrew, her expression guarded, but remained standing by the cabin door.

Karidian turned steady, luminous eyes on Kirk. He said, "What is it you want, Captain?"

"I want a straight answer to a straight question," Kirk said. "And I promise you this: You won't be harmed aboard this ship, and you'll be dealt with fairly when you leave it."

Karidian only nodded, as if he had expected nothing else. He was certainly intimidating. Finally Kirk said:

"I suspect you, Mr. Karidian. You know that. I believe the greatest performance of your life is the part you're acting out offstage."

Karidian smiled, a little sourly. "Each man in his time plays many parts."

"I'm concerned with only one. Tell me this: Are you Kodos the Executioner?"

Karidian looked toward his daughter, but he did not really seem to see her; his eyes were open, but shuttered, like a cat's.

"That was a long time ago," he said. "Back then I was a young character actor, touring the Earth colonies... As you see, I'm still doing it."

"That's not an answer," Kirk said.

"What did you expect? Were I Kodos, I would have the blood of thousands on my hands. Should I confess to a stranger, after twenty years of fleeing much more organized justice? Whatever Kodos was in those days, I have never heard it said that he was a fool."

"I have done you a favor," Kirk said. "And I have promised to treat you fairly. That's not an ordinary promise. I am the captain of this ship, and whatever justice there is aboard it is in my hands."

"I see you differently. You stand before me as the perfect symbol of our technological society: mechanized, electronicized, uniformed... and not precisely human. I hate machinery, Captain. It has done away with humanity—the striving of men to achieve greatness through their own resources. That's why I am a live actor, still, instead of a shadow on a three-V film."

"The lever is a tool," Kirk said. "We have new tools, but great men still strive, and don't feel outclassed. Wicked men use the tools to murder, like Kodos; but that doesn't make the tools wicked. Guns don't shoot people. Only men do."

"Kodos," Karidian said, "whoever he was, made decisions of life and death. Some had to die that others could live. That is the lot of kings, and the cross of kings. And probably of commanders, too—otherwise why should you be here now?"

"I don't remember ever having killed four thousand innocent people."

"I don't remember it either. But I do remember that another four thousand were saved because of it. Were I to direct a play about Kodos, that is the first thing I would bear in mind."

"It wasn't a play," Kirk said. "I was there. I saw it happen. And since then, all the surviving witnesses have been systematically murdered, except two... or possibly, three. One of my officers has been poisoned. I may be next. And here you are, a man of whom we have no record until some nine years ago—and positively identified, positively, no matter how mistakenly, by the late Dr. Leighton. Do you think I can ignore all that?"

"No, certainly not," Karidian said. "But that is your role. I have mine. I have played many." He looked down at his worn hands. "Sooner or later, the blood thins, the body ages, and finally one is grateful for a failing memory. I no longer treasure life—not even my own. Death for me will be a release from ritual. I am old and tired, and the past is blank."

"And that's your only answer?"

"I'm afraid so, Captain. Did you ever get everything you wanted? No, nobody does. And if you did, you might be sorry."

Kirk shrugged and turned away. He found Lenore staring at him, but there was nothing he could do for her, either. He went out.

She followed him. In the corridor on the other side of the door, she said in a cold whisper: "You are a machine. And with a big bloody stain of cruelty on your metal hide. You could have spared him."

"If he's Kodos," Kirk said, equally quietly, "then I've already shown him more mercy than he deserves. If he isn't, then we'll put you ashore at Eta Benecia, with no harm done."

"Who are you," Lenore said in a dangerous voice, "to say what harm is done?"

"Who do I have to be?"

She seemed to be about to answer; cold fire raged in her eyes. But at the same moment, the door slid open behind her and Karidian stood there, no longer so tall or so impressive as he had been before. Tears began to run down over her cheeks; she reached for his shoulders, her head drooping.

"Father . . . father . . ."

"Never mind," Karidian said gently, regaining a little of his stature. "It's already all over. I am thy father's spirit, doomed for a certain time to walk the night—"

"Hush!"

Feeling like six different varieties of monster, Kirk left them alone together.

For the performance, the briefing room had been re-dressed into a small theater, and cameras were spotted here and there so that the play could be seen on inter-com screens elsewhere in the ship for the part of the crew that had to remain on duty. The lights were already down. Kirk was late, as usual; he was just settling into his seat—as captain he was entitled to a front row chair and had had no hesitation about claiming it—when the curtains parted and Lenore came through them, in the flowing costume of Ophelia, white with make-up.

She said in a clear, almost gay voice: "Tonight the Karidian Players present *Hamlet*—another in a series of living plays in space—dedicated to the tradition of the classic theater, which we believe will never die. *Hamlet* is a violent play about a violent time, when life was cheap and ambition was God. It is also a timeless play, about personal guilt, doubt, indecision, and the thin line between Justice and Vengeance."

She vanished, leaving Kirk brooding. Nobody needed to be introduced to *Hamlet;* that speech had been aimed directly at him. He did not need the reminder, either, but he had got it nonetheless.

The curtains parted and the great, chilling opening began. Kirk lost most of it, since McCoy chose that moment to arrive and seat himself next to Kirk with a great bustle.

"Here we are, here we are," McCoy muttered. "In the long history of medicine no doctor has ever caught the curtain of a play."

"Shut up," Kirk said, *sotto voce.* "You had plenty of notice."

"Yes, but nobody told me I'd lose a patient at the last minute."

"Somebody dead?"

"No, no. Lieutenant Daiken absconded out of sick bay, that's all. I suppose he wanted to see the play too."

"It's being piped into sick bay!"

"I know that. Pipe down, will you? How can I hear if you keep mumbling?"

Swearing silently, Kirk got up and went out. Once he was in the corridor, he went to the nearest open line and ordered a search; but it turned out that McCoy already had one going.

Routine, Kirk decided, was not enough. Daiken's entire family had been destroyed on Tarsus . . . and somebody had tried to kill him. This was no time to take even the slightest chance; with the play going on, not only Karidian, but the whole ship was vulnerable to any access of passion . . . or vengeance.

"Red security alert," Kirk said. "Search every inch, including cargo."

Getting confirmation, he went back into the converted briefing room. He was still not satisfied, but there was nothing more he could do now.

His ears were struck by a drum beat. The stage was dim, lit only by a wash of red, and the characters playing Marcellus and Horatio were just going off. Evidently the play had already reached Act One, Scene 5. The figure of the ghost materialized in the red beam and raised its arm, beckoning to Hamlet, but Hamlet refused to follow. The ghost—Karidian—beckoned again, and the drum beat heightened in intensity.

Kirk could think of nothing but that Karidian was now an open target. He circled the rapt audience quickly and silently, making for the rear of the stage.

"Speak," Hamlet said. "I'll go no further."

"Mark me," said Karidian hollowly.

"I will."

"My hour is almost come, when I to sulphurous and tormenting flames must render up myself—"

There was Daiken, crouching in the wings. He was already leveling a phaser at Karidian.

"—and you must seek revenge—"

"Daiken!" Kirk said. There was no help for it; he had to call across the stage. The dialogues intercut.

"I am thy father's spirit, doomed for a certain term to walk the night—"

"He murdered my father," Daiken said. "And my mother."

"—And for the day confined to fast in fires, Till the foul crimes done in my days—"

"Get back to sick bay!"

"I know. I saw. He murdered them."

"—are burnt and purged away."

The audience had begun to murmur; they could hear every word. So could Karidian. He looked off toward Daiken, but the light was too bad for him to see anything. In a shaken voice, he tried to go on.

"I . . . I could a tale unfold whose lightest word—"

"You could be wrong. Don't throw your life away on a mistake."

"—would t-tear up thy soul, freeze thy young blood—"

"Daiken, give me that weapon."

"No."

Several people in the audience were standing now, and Kirk could see a few security guards moving cautiously down the sidelines. They would be too late; Daiken had a dead bead on Karidian.

Then the scenery at the back tore, and Lenore came out. Her eyes were bright and feverish, and in her hand she carried an absurdly long dagger.

"It's over!" she said in a great, theatrical voice. "Never mind, father, I'm strong! Come, ye spirits of the air, unsex me now! Hie thee hither, that in the porches of thine ear—"

"Child, child!"

She could not hear him. She was the mad Ophelia; but the lines were Lady Macbeth's.

"All the ghosts are dead. Who would have thought they had so much blood in 'em? I've freed you, father. I've taken the blood away from you. Had he not so much resembled my father as he slept, I'd have done it—"

"No!" Karidian said, his voice choked with horror. "You've left me nothing! You were untouched by what I did, you weren't even born! I wanted to leave you something clean—"

"Balsam! I've given you everything! You're safe, no one can touch you! See Banquo there, the Caesar, even he can't touch you! This castle hath a pleasant seat."

Kirk went out onto the stage, watching the security guards out of the corner of his eyes. Daiken seemed to be frozen by the action under the lights, but his gun still had not wavered.

"That's enough," Kirk said. "Come with me, both of you."

Karidian turned to him, spreading his hands wide. "Captain," he said. "Try to understand. I was a soldier in a great cause. There were things that had to be done—hard things, terrible things. You know the price of that; you too are a captain."

"Stop it, father," Lenore said, in a spuriously rational voice. "There is nothing to explain."

"There is. Murder. Flight. Suicide. Madness. And still the price is not enough; my daughter has killed too."

"For you! For you! I saved you!"

"For the price of seven innocent men," Kirk said.

"Innocent?" Lenore gave a great theatrical laugh, like a coloratura playing Medea. "Innocent! They saw! They were guilty!"

"That's enough, Lenore," Kirk said. "The play is over. It was over twenty years ago. Are you coming with me, or do I have to drag you?"

"Better go," Daiken's voice said from the wings. He stood up and came forward into the light, the gun still leveled. "I wasn't going to be so merciful, but we've had enough madness. Thanks, Captain."

Lenore spun on him. With a movement like a flash of lightning, she snatched the gun away from him.

"Stand back!" she screamed. "Stand back, everyone! The play goes on!"

"No!" Karidian cried out hoarsely. "In the name of God, child—"

"Captain Caesar! You could have had Egypt! Beware the Ides of March!"

She pointed the gun at Kirk and pulled the trigger. But fast as she was in her madness, Karidian was even quicker. The beam struck him squarely on the chest. He fell silently.

Lenore wailed like a lost kitten and dropped to her knees beside him. The security guards stampeded onto the stage, but Kirk waved them back.

"Father!" Lenore crooned. "Father! Oh proud death, what feast is toward in thine eternal cell, that thou such a prince at a shot so bloodily has struck!" She began to laugh again. "The cue, father, the cue! No time to sleep! The play! The play's the thing, wherein we'll catch the conscience of the king..."

Gentle hands drew her away. In Kirk's ear, McCoy's voice said: "And in the long run, she didn't even get the lines right."

"Take care of her," Kirk said tonelessly. "Kodos is dead...but I think she may walk in her sleep."